THIS PUFFIN MODERN CLASSIC
BELONGS TO

_____

PUFFIN MODERN CLASSICS

Cue for Treason

Geoffrey Trease was born in Nottingham in 1909. He had his first book published in 1934 and went on to write more than 100 books for both children and adults. He is best known for his children's historical novels such as *Cue for Treason*, about which a famous critic wrote 'a new era in the adventure story opened'. *Cue for Treason* was written in the anxious opening months of the Second World War. At the time Geoffrey Trease did not know whether he would be called up to join the army before he finished it, or still be alive when it was published. It came out in 1940, but all warehouse stocks were destroyed in the London Blitz. It was also published in New York and Toronto and, as soon as paper became available again after the war, it was reissued in Britain. It has remained in print ever since. Geoffrey Trease died in 1998.

GEOFFREY TREASE

Cue for Treason

ILLUSTRATED BY ZENA FLAX

PUFFIN BOOKS

Published by the Penguin Group
Penguin Books Ltd, 80 Strand, London WC2R 0RL, England
Penguin Group (USA) Inc., 375 Hudson Street, New York, New York 10014, USA
Penguin Group (Canada), 90 Eglinton Avenue East, Suite 700, Toronto, Ontario, Canada M4P 2Y3
(a division of Pearson Penguin Canada Inc.)
Penguin Ireland, 25 St Stephen's Green, Dublin 2, Ireland (a division of Penguin Books Ltd)
Penguin Group (Australia), 250 Camberwell Road, Camberwell, Victoria 3124, Australia
(a division of Pearson Australia Group Pty Ltd)
Penguin Books India Pvt Ltd, 11 Community Centre, Panchsheel Park,
New Delhi – 110 017, India
Penguin Group (NZ), cnr Airborne and Rosedale Roads, Albany, Auckland 1310, New Zealand
(a division of Pearson New Zealand Ltd)
Penguin Books (South Africa) (Pty) Ltd, 24 Sturdee Avenue, Rosebank,
Johannesburg 2196, South Africa

Penguin Books Ltd, Registered Offices: 80 Strand, London WC2R 0RL, England

puffinbooks.com

First published by Blackwell 1940
Published in Puffin Books 1965
Published in Puffin Modern Classics 2009
002

Copyright © Geoffrey Trease, 1940
All rights reserved

The moral right of the author has been asserted

Set in 11/16.25pt Palatino by Palimpsest Book Production Limited, Grangemouth, Stirlingshire
Made and printed in England by Clays Ltd, St Ives plc

British Library Cataloguing in Publication Data
A CIP catalogue record for this book is available from the British Library

ISBN: 978-0-141-32570-5

www.greenpenguin.co.uk

ALWAYS LEARNING   **PEARSON**

Introduction

by Julia Eccleshare

Puffin Modern Classics series editor

How vividly the past comes to life in this thrilling adventure story! Far, far from the dusty textbook view of history, *Cue for Treason* is an action-packed spy thriller in which two children show bravery and independence when they get caught up in a traitor's plot and must turn their hands to espionage.

In a story that embraces the excitement of Elizabethan theatre, the politics of the times and the domestic details of long, long ago, Geoffrey Trease creates a past, which, while rich in contemporary detail, feels as accessible and tangible as any modern-day setting. Lacking the technology on which we rely so heavily, communication is very personal and trust is paramount. Death is never far from those who take risks and the two children are willing to take more than their fair share.

Stepping back in time is effortless. Although the details are unfamiliar, what Trease describes was real once and he inhabits it absolutely. By weaving in actual historical figures – such as Shakespeare, who has a starring role, and, of course, Queen Elizabeth I herself, along with her wise servant and spymaster, Sir Robert Cecil – we are readily transported into their world, and eager and able to play our part in it.

Through its central characters, *Cue for Treason* shows the value of independence, courage and a clear view of right and wrong. Without being smug or preachy about what they believe in, Peter and Kit are determined to save their queen. Their courage is infectious; all readers will happily follow them.

Although set in olden times, there is nothing old-fashioned about *Cue for Treason*. It is an exciting story that encompasses danger and intrigue and some truly warm-hearted characters. Geoffrey Trease brings Elizabethan England to life while fostering pride in serving your country.

Long live Peter and Kit! And long live good Queen Elizabeth!

Contents

1.

Dawn is Dangerous

I asked, weren't we taking the pistol, or anyhow the long, murderous-looking pike which has hung across our broad kitchen chimney ever since I can remember? I was disappointed when my father whispered, 'No,' and more than disappointed – in fact, I felt mad – when Tom said, in that sneering superior way that elder brothers have:

'What do you think this is, kid – a raid against the Scots? Or do you fancy you're marching against the Spaniards?'

I was glad it was pitch dark in the kitchen where we stood whispering. There wasn't a glimmer from the fire, though the fire has never gone out in my lifetime, nor for a few years before that. But, as usual, Mother had covered it with slabs of black, damp peat before we went to bed, and it wouldn't show a gleam till morning, when one poke would stir it into a cheerful blaze.

I was glad it was dark, so that Tom couldn't see my face. I was getting tired of the way he made fun of me.

Why shouldn't we go armed? There *was* danger in what we had decided to do. Otherwise, why were we creeping out of the house in the middle of the night, like foxes round a sheep-pen?

'Leave the boy alone,' said my father in his deep whisper. 'No more words till we're clear of home, or we'll be waking your mother and the girls.'

'Doesn't Mother –' I began.

'Sh!' said Tom importantly, like the beadle in church on Sundays. I had the satisfaction of tapping his shin as we groped our way through the door, and he daren't say a word. He was only sixteen, after all, and Dad would have leathered him as readily as he would me, if need arose.

It was lighter when we got outside. The full moon had risen now above the crest of the fells, and all the upper air was bright, though our valley was still like a pool of darkness. The silver light slanted across the valley, high above our heads, and struck the wild precipices of Blencathra mountain, showing up the black gulleys as though their shadows were splashed on with ink. Every minute, as the moon climbed higher, the shadow-line dropped a little down the mountainside, like water ebbing away, and I knew that by the time we got to Sir Philip's wall there would be ample light for what we had to do.

The dog rose silently from the threshold as we stepped into the soft midsummer air. Not a bark, not a growl – he knew our steps. My father hesitated, then grunted something, and Snap's tail drooped. He gave a long, soft sigh, and curled up again, burying his nose in his bushy tail.

If Snap had gone with us that night, as he wanted to, I should never have come into the peril of death, and this story would never have been told. But it's no good crying over spilt milk, and perhaps it wasn't such a bad thing after all.

We walked down in single file, without speaking a word. There's a stream at the bottom – becks we call them in Cumberland – and you cross it by flat granite slabs, which in winter are often under water, though on a July night like that they stood a foot clear of the frothy surface. When we got that far, we knew the rush and gurgle of the beck would drown our voices, so we could talk without whispering.

'Your mother would only worry,' said my father, 'in any case, the fewer who know about tonight's work the better. Then, if questions are asked, the fewer lies will need to be told.'

I felt rather pleased when he said that, about 'the fewer who knew the better'. Though I was only fourteen, I had been counted in with the men. They could say what they liked, but there *was* a certain amount of danger. Sir Philip was a bad enemy to cross, though up to that time none of us knew just how bad an enemy he could be.

Anyhow, it doesn't do to believe my father always when he says a thing isn't dangerous. See him going up a crag to rescue a stranded sheep! See him squaring up to some drunken German miner in Keswick market-place – some fellow twice his size, jabbering his foreign lingo and waving a great dagger, like as not.

When you see my father's red beard jut out a shade more boldly than usual, and when you hear him chuckle down in his broad chest, and murmur, 'I'm all right, leave this to me; there's no danger', then you can get ready for some excitement.

Nothing *should* have happened that night. The secret had been well kept.

Not even Tom knew what was in the wind till my father roused us just after midnight, telling us to take our clogs in our hands and creep downstairs. But we guessed at once what it was all about.

We'd been a happy enough family in our valley till young Sir Philip Morton had inherited his grand-father's estate a couple of years before. Brownriggs,

Bells, Atkinsons, Hudsons, Cockbains – we were all old farming families, who had kept our sheep on the fells since Domesday Book or the founding of Rome or, for all I know, since the Flood itself. We held our land direct from the Crown, and all the rent we paid was to fight the Scots if they came over. We weren't gentry, we were yeomen – 'statesmen' or 'estatesmen' we call ourselves up there – but we were independent people, not caring much for man or devil. Certainly we didn't care anything for a young knight who put scent on his handkerchief and didn't know one end of a Herdwick sheep from another.

But Sir Philip soon showed us that he wasn't a soft young man. In fact, he was extremely hard. We were sorry for the lowland farmers who rented lands from him, for their rents began to go up like rockets. Then he turned his attention to us.

He couldn't hit us so easily. But there was one way.

Down in the valley, by the river, the meadows have been common land since time immemorial. I don't say they belong to nobody – they belong to *us*, Brownriggs and Bells and the rest of the families who've farmed Lonsdale all these hundreds of years. And Heaven help the man who puts a stone wall round them and calls them his – even if he has money and men in livery and a 'Sir' in front of his name.

That's what Sir Philip did that summer.

His men came one day at dawn and started on the job. Most of our men were away up the fells – I was off to school at Keswick myself – and when Mr Atkinson went down to warn them off, they threatened to throw the poor old man into the Greta. So the wall was done, almost, before our people had time to turn round and discuss the matter. They complained afterwards, of course, but a late complaint is like cold porridge, precious little use.

Sir Philip snapped his fingers at us. Asked us where our title-deeds were, waved a roll of yellow Latin documents which might have meant anything, and `challenged us to take the matter to court.

No one wanted to do that. We hadn't much money for lawyers, and we didn't trust them either. Besides, said my father, why go cap in hand to a bench of judges to beg back the land which was ours and always had been?

That was why, that night, the dale was full of moving shadows.

From every farmstead the men and boys were marching down to the meeting-place. And the meeting-place was Sir Philip Morton's wall.

It shone white and new in the moonlight, which by now had slanted down far enough to reach it. You could see the faces of the waiting men, too, white and drained of their usual ruddiness. Their teeth flashed as they greeted us with a laugh and a word. It was almost like a meeting to hunt foxes, only there were no hounds.

My father cocked his eye at the moon, now sailing as serenely as the *Golden Hind* across the great expanse of sky.

'Just nice time we've got, friends, before morning. Now, before we set to work, let me remind the young 'uns, specially, what we have decided to do.'

We all clustered round, and he made us all swear a solemn oath we'd tell no one a single word about the night's doings. Sir Philip could do nothing to the whole village, but if he got proof against one or two individual men, he'd try to get his revenge on them.

'All stand together, and keep mum,' my father ended. With that, he spat on his hands very deliberately, strode up to the wall, and pushed at the top row. I shall never forget the sound as the small flat slabs rattled and clinked to the ground. The die was cast.

Then we all set to work with a will to throw down Sir Philip's wonderful wall.

It was a dry wall, of course, such as we build in our part of the world when we make a pen for sheep. There was no mortar binding the rough stones together. They were fitted carefully – it's a real craft, building those walls – and at proper intervals you put in binding stones of the right size and shape, to hold the lot in place. A well-built wall can stand the winter gales and the weight of a great snowdrift. The walls my grandad built under Blencathra will be standing long after I'm dead and gone.

Sir Philip's won't, though!

There must have been thirty or forty of us out that night, and we all worked as if it were haymaking-time and a thunderstorm just coming up from Derwentwater way. My own hands were soon bleeding – I'd torn a nail on the rough stones. You never heard such a bump and clatter as that wall went down, all along the line. It was a great game for us all, knocking it over in heaps. Even the older men were laughing like boys at school.

'Here, Peter,' my father said, 'run up to the road, there's a good lad, and keep an eye open for anyone coming. Mr Bell's a wee bit nervous; he thinks we ought to have a scout on the watch.'

'What does he think this is?' I said, imitating Tom's voice. 'A raid against the Scots?'

All the same, I wasn't sorry to go. My hands were hurting, and knocking a wall down gets monotonous after half an hour.

I walked up from the river to the road. I could see a goodish way towards Keswick – the road wound white and bright, except where the moonbeams were broken by black clumps of oak and ash and birch. I couldn't see so far towards Penrith, for there was a bend hiding the distance. I walked there, and looked eastwards. Now I could see a clear mile or two of the road climbing up the hem of Blencathra, which I still think is the noblest mountain in the world. I ought to have stayed at that bend, for it was that way that Sir Philip's new manor-house stood; I could see the moonlight flashing on its wonderful glass windows, though it was every bit of three miles away. But I wanted to stay where I could see the others, and hear the jokes they shouted to one another, and watch that wonderful wall going down as though it were the rampart of Jericho itself.

So after one glance to make sure that there was no living soul on the road to eastward – which was about as much use as a silk slipper in a snowstorm – I turned and walked back.

Soldiers say that dawn is a dangerous time. I have heard that from men who have fought in Ireland and the Low Countries and in the steaming forests of the Spanish Main. It's the time when sentries get slack and their eyelids droop, and a wise enemy chooses his moment to launch a surprise attack.

It was getting towards dawn. The moon would soon be down. The rich blue colour was draining out of the eastern sky, and the mist was coming up from the meadows, so that I could see only the heads and shoulders of the men standing in their long line, each a few paces from his neighbour. High above us, the mountain mists were drawn close round the peaks like the curtains of a four-poster bed.

The wall was so low I could no longer see it. But I saw young Dick Hudson jump over it with a cry of derision, and I thought of the story we read in the old histories of Rome, of how Remus jumped scornfully over the first low wall of the city. Romulus killed *him*, and I expect Sir Philip would cheerfully have killed Dick Hudson if he'd seen him at that moment. But Sir Philip wasn't there, and he'd never know . . .

When people asked who'd overthrown that wall, we were all going to say it must be the work of the Devil. The Devil has a great reputation for destroying what honest men would be glad to see out of the way!

So the dawn drew near, and danger too, if I'd only known it, and not been so occupied watching them scatter the last stones, right and left, in the long wet grass.

I felt, rather than heard, the coming of the horsemen.

They weren't riding the sunbaked earth and rock of the road itself – they galloped almost silently along the green verge, so that there was no loud ring of hooves to set the valley echoing from fell to fell, but only a dull, regular vibration.

I wasn't aware of them till they swept round the bend, not a hundred yards from where I was standing.

It was Sir Philip in front; I knew him by his grey mount. There were a dozen or more behind him, strung out head to tail, head to tail, and every rider with a sword or pistol or both.

I gaped at them for a half-second, I was so dumbfounded. Then, as my big mouth was conveniently open, I stuck in two fingers and whistled. *That* set the echoes going all right.

It was everyone for himself then. Luckily for me, there were plenty of rocks heaped about on the steep hillside above the road, and once among these I should be safe. I skipped into the shelter just before the cavalcade reached me. Then I was tempted by some devil I couldn't resist; I turned round with a piece of rock in my fist and shied it straight at Sir Philip. I don't think it touched either man or horse, they were travelling too fast, but it made the horse shy, and threw the men behind into temporary confusion.

'There's one of 'em, sir!' a man shouted, and flung up his pistol. The muzzle flamed in the twilight, and it is a wonder my story didn't finish there and then. I felt the bullet whizz through my hair – which was standing on end, I expect, for I'd never been fired at before. I'm not exaggerating. The cap was blown clean from my

head, and fell somewhere among the rocks, where I'd neither time nor inclination to stay and look for it.

Instead, I hared up that mountain as though all the hounds in Cumberland were trailing me. Only when my heart felt as though it would burst through my skin did I drop breathless on my belly, on an overhanging slab of granite, and look back into the valley.

Of my father and brother and the neighbours there wasn't a sign. They'd vanished like June snow. The daylight, growing every moment, showed only Sir Philip and his servants, clustered glumly round the ruins of the wall.

I slipped home by a roundabout way. I shall always remember that summer morning, with the sun bounding up between Great Mell and Great Dod, and the wild roses out along the Greta, and the hay that had been cut yesterday so rich and scented on the air.

I enjoyed it especially because, if that bullet had been an inch or two lower, I should never have seen the sun rise over Lonsdale again. I never thought as I jumped the beck and went up to our house that it would be many a long day before I *did* see it again. To tell you the truth, I was thinking mainly of breakfast.

2.

Escape

School was at six in the morning. Seven o'clock in winter – if it was possible to get through the snow at all.

The grammar school was down at Crosthwaite, close under the shadow of the church tower. It was a broad, flat valley thereabouts. When the floods were out, Derwent-water joined hands with the other lake, Bassenthwaite, so that the church and school, standing on a narrow tongue of higher ground, were almost islanded by the white silent waters. It was every yard of five miles from home, mostly downhill. I had a shaggy old pony, Nathaniel, and I always enjoyed the ride. It took me right through the middle of Keswick town, so I saw plenty of life every day – for which some of the older people envied me, stuck away as they were in the lonely valleys and seeing never a fresh face from one week's end to another.

It would have been fun to have told my friends about the excitements of the night, but I remembered the promise we'd all given not to breathe a word. That didn't stop me making up, just in my own mind, a story of how I had defied Sir Philip from the top of a perilous crag, and then hurled a hundredweight boulder at him, tumbling horse and man into the river. Of course, the boys wouldn't have believed me, but they'd have clapped when I acted the scene to them, imitating Sir Philip's haughtiness and my own heroic gestures.

Anyhow, I promised myself, I'll go back there tonight when the coast's clear and find my cap. A cap with a bullet-hole – *that'll* be something to show at school, something they'll have to believe in. They all know that green cap of mine, and it has my name in it, anyhow, so they can't pretend I've got hold of someone else's. I'll invent a good yarn to explain that cap, I thought gleefully . . .

It was a pity I never had time. It would have come in mighty useful.

That morning passed by as all other mornings had before. We sat round the school hall on our various benches, learning our grammar and writing, our Latin and Greek literature or our Hebrew, according to our age. There were only a few boys older than I. They were fifteen or sixteen, and nearly ready to go away to the Queen's College at Oxford. The master wanted me to do that too, but I could never quite decide. I wanted to see the outside world, but I did not want to leave the farm.

That day decided one question, anyhow.

We stopped work at eleven, and had two hours, midday, to eat the dinner we'd brought and play games. I remember Tim Moore and I went off to the lake for a swim, for it had turned out one of those sweaty summer days, when the mountains don't look real and the air hangs in the great bowl of the valley like stale water. We took Nathaniel and rode by turns, for Tim lived in the town and hadn't a pony himself.

We had our swim, and the sun dried us, and I was just pulling my shirt over my head again when young George Bell came running along the lake-shore, waving and shouting.

'Peter Brownrigg!'

'Hullo!' I said.

'The master wants you,' he said, all panting.

I looked at the sun and guessed it was just after twelve, nearly an hour before lessons began again. 'He can wait,' I said.

'That's right,' said Tim, with a grin. 'Say you looked everywhere, but you couldn't find us.'

'No; you'd better come now. There's some men asking for you.'

'Men?' I echoed.

'Two men,' he said. 'One of them's the constable, but I don't know the other. They'd got that green cap of yours –'

As soon as he mentioned the green cap I knew that it was serious. I must have gone very white. Tim stared at me.

'What've you been up to, Peter, my lad?'

'Nothing,' I said, which wasn't at all true, but I spoke mechanically, for I was thinking hard. I was frightened – and I'm not ashamed to admit it. So would you have been. They'd got that cap of mine, and they knew whose it was. I didn't know what the exact penalty was for throwing a rock at a man, but as the man was one of the leading gentlemen in the district I could imagine it would be something heavy. If it wasn't hanging it might be prison, with possibly earcropping or nose-slitting or flogging into the bargain. And the chief witnesses would all be Sir Philip's men, who would be ready to swear to anything their master said.

My first thought was what any other boy's first thought would have been: home. It's a kind of instinct you don't lose till you get older. While you're a boy, you somehow imagine there's no trouble your father can't save you from if he tries.

I caught hold of Nathaniel and jumped on his back.

'I'm going home,' I said, 'but don't tell them so. Georgie, *you* say you couldn't find me. And Tim, say I left you by Friar's Crag.'

They both stared at me, goggle-eyed. 'You're going to play truant?' said George. 'The old man'll have the hide off your back.'

'It's not him I'm afraid of,' I said, trying to sound very grand and dramatic. 'It's the sheriff – and maybe the hangman!' I wasted no more time, but dug my heels into Nathaniel's tubby sides and galloped away.

That was all very fine – till I was out of sight of the boys. But as Nat's gallop dropped to a canter, his canter to a trot, and, as the road grew steeper, his trot to a plodding walk, I began to feel less and less of a hero.

Here was a nice mess! Just my luck! Of all the twenty or thirty who'd helped to demolish Sir Philip's wall, I was the only one they had traced, and actually I had done less than all the others. But then I'd committed an assault . . . thrown a stone, which had missed. It didn't sound much. I'd thrown plenty of stones at people when I was smaller, and I'd often hit them, but I'd never had the constable after me before. This, though, was Sir Philip Morton, and it made a difference.

How I cursed poor old Nathaniel as he ambled up the long hill! He was doing his best, and the sun was scorching us both, but I was terrified lest I should be caught before I reached home. Once I heard hooves and looked back, but it was only a gentleman from Keswick, who passed me with his usual nod. He at any rate hadn't heard yet of my misdoings.

It's usually a pleasant moment when you turn off the high road along the rough trail which leads up your own valley to home and nowhere else. But never before had I felt so glad to see the steep fells give back on either hand to show the green nook of Lonsdale, with the becks racing down like spilt milk and the smoke going up from our own chimneys and those of our neighbours above and below.

I was afraid I should have to look for my father on the fell; but no, he was there, standing in the porch with his hand shading his eyes as Nathaniel came splashing up through the beck.

'God be thanked!' I heard him say, and that brought my mother out, wiping her eyes on her blue linen apron. I could see they knew all about it.

'I'm sorry,' was all I could say. 'Don't worry.'

'You must get away from here,' my father said, as if

he'd got it thought out. 'It'll blow over, lad, but you'll be better away from home for a bit. Are they close after you?'

'I don't know how close,' I said. 'I'm safe for an hour.'

'Where can he *go*?' Mother wailed. 'If my mother were still alive at Carlisle, we could have sent him there, but as it is . . .' She looked at my father. 'Wouldn't it be better for him to stay and face them? I'm sure he's done no wrong, no more than any of them, and there's not a man in the dale who won't swear what a good boy he is.'

'You don't know the law,' my father said grimly. 'No, they mustn't get hold of him now, while Sir Philip's in his mad mood. Besides, we owe it to our neighbours to get him away. If the court lays hands on him, they'll question him about his companions at the time.'

That set my mother off again, weeping, and I wasn't far off myself, for I knew very well what sort of questioning he meant. I knew I couldn't stand torture. If the law let them do that, even a little of it, I knew I should blurt out the names of every man and boy who'd been there that night.

There was nothing for it but to clear out before they tracked me home.

'I'll be all right,' I comforted my mother. 'I'll get out

of the district; I'll slip across into Scotland perhaps; I'll get work, and I'll send word to you that I'm all right. Then in a few months, maybe, I shall be able to come back, and the whole thing be forgotten.'

'It's the best thing,' said my father.

He went to where the money was kept, and counted out five shillings.* 'That'll keep you going for a few days,' he said. 'I wish it could be more, but . . .' I knew. Times were hard, and we never handled much cash in Lonsdale. My mother brought me a couple of loaves, cheese, and oatmeal cakes, and a piece of cold mutton, big enough for three.

We wasted no time in talk, for we knew that at any moment we might see the horsemen riding up the dale to fetch me.

I wouldn't take Nathaniel, for they would have caught me at once if I'd stuck to the road, and I couldn't have borne to sell the old boy in Penrith. Instead, I decided to make for Penrith on foot, across the fells, where there would be ample cover from pursuit. There was a market at Penrith next day, and amid the crowds of strangers I should be able to avoid notice and perhaps – who knew? – find some work to help me get out of Cumberland.

---

* Money then was worth roughly ten times as much as today.

I never saw my brother to say good-bye, for he was up the fell. My sisters were cheese-making. They wept buckets over me; I'd never realized how fond of me my sisters were until that day. Then I tore myself away, shouldered my bundle with a few clothes, and started up the beck to the high crest of the moor.

Five minutes later, when I was right up in the tough grass and the heather, I looked back and saw my dale below, with the houses like little grey boxes, right and left of the brown lane. And along that lane, just turned off the high road, came two riders, crawling along like two silly, bright-backed beetles.

I laughed, though I didn't feel at all like laughing, and went tramping on up the mountain.

I'd always wanted to see the outside world, I'd always wanted adventure, and now I was going to get it with a vengeance.

3.

Peril at Penrith

No one followed me up the mountain. I walked for an hour or two along the northern slopes of Blencathra, and saw no living thing but a cluster of red deer on the far skyline of Skiddaw Forest, and an eagle circling lazily in the thick sky. Late in the afternoon I came to the Stronghold.

We used to play there, when we were smaller and still enjoyed war-games like English-and-Scots or English-and-Spanish. It was a long way from home, but there was no place like it, and I've spent many a day there. There was a small lake or tarn, black and bottomless, and the precipices rose all round it in the shape of a horseshoe, except on the eastern side, where the ground fell away, and a little stream came bubbling out of the tarn to join the Glendermakin River in the valley below.

The Stronghold was a natural hiding-place among the giant rocks that littered the lakeside. There was one over-hanging boulder under which half a dozen of us could have lain and slept, bone-dry, through the wettest night. Other big stones lay round in a rough circle, which we called the 'courtyard'. By heaping up a few smaller stones, which we could lift ourselves, we turned the rocks into continuous ramparts.

We got the idea of a stronghold from the old peel-tower which stood some way down the valley. In grandfather's time, all the wealthier people lived in peel-towers of that kind, because you never knew when the Scots might come pouring over the Border on one of their raiding expeditions. But there had been no such raid since I was born, and some of the local squires were giving up their 'peels' and building ordinary houses.

That's what Sir Philip Morton had done. He'd built himself a fine new mansion down by the Greta, with tall chimneys and windows with hundreds of little diamond panes. The old house – the peel-tower – now stood empty and tumbling into ruin. It was an oblong, three-storey affair, with tiny windows and none at all (let alone a door) on the ground-level. To enter, you had to climb a flight of stone steps outside and, if the massive oak door was then barred in your face, you weren't any forrader.

Like a little fort the Mortons' peel-tower was, with its battlemented roof and its little corner turret for the watchman and its iron basket to hold the warning beacon. But it must have been a bleak, gloomy box to live in, standing so high and so far from roads and houses, so I don't wonder that Sir Philip had given it up and built something more comfortable.

Well, as I say, late that afternoon I came to the Stronghold we boys had made in imitation of the peel. I felt it was a safe spot to hide overnight, because it was so seldom people went up there.

Sure enough I found the Stronghold just as we'd left it three summers before, when we grew too old for the game. A hundred drenching storms had washed away the black circle of our fires, but nothing else was changed. The sheep's skull still grinned from 'the topmast battlement' – we used to pretend it was a traitor's who had committed high treason against the Queen – and there were all our initials, a little fainter perhaps, scratched on the rock below.

I had to get to Penrith, and out of the country where I was known. From the Stronghold to Penrith was twelve miles as the crow flies, and rather more by the winding road, which would be safe enough after dark. I reckoned I could walk it in five hours. If I stayed in the Stronghold and rested till nearly midnight, I could do the journey under the moon, and land in the town as soon as it was properly astir.

I can't say I enjoyed that long evening in the Stronghold. The sun was soon hidden by the crags which rise round the tarn, but long after I was sunk in a gloomy pool of shadow, I could see the beams warm and friendly on the upper slopes of White Horse Bent and Souther Fell. It was as if I had dropped out of the day hours too soon. Yet it didn't get dark; I began to feel it never *would* get dark. The sunset went on for ever. And there was nothing to do, once I had eaten a dismal supper of cold meat and bread, with icy water from the beck. I was in a hurry to be off, but I daren't start till dark.

Never before had I been up at the Stronghold either alone or so late. It was very eerie. As the twilight gathered, the dead place seemed to come alive. The crags seemed to move. Once something went flapping thunderously overhead, and there was a long, harsh screech which went echoing all round the rock-faces. Even the beck, so friendly a thing in daylight, seemed to be chuckling in a new and unpleasant fashion. I would have risked a fire, but I had nothing to burn and nothing to light it with. I tried to snatch some sleep, but the ground was too hard, and if the best goosefeather bed had been offered me I should have been too excited to close my eyes.

When I judged it to be about eleven – it was hard to tell, for the moon wasn't up yet – I could stand the place no longer. I shouldered my bundle and groped my way along the mountainside till I reached the high saddle which joins Scales Fell to Souther Fell. Luckily I knew every inch of this ground, and, though I tumbled twice in the darkness, I knew there was no danger of broken necks along this way. Soon a beck sprang from the ground below me, and, using it as a guide, I came quickly down to the Penrith road, just where it crosses the Glendermakin.

It was good to feel the hard road under my feet again – but mighty hard it felt by the time I sighted the red ramparts of Penrith Castle standing up on its hill.

Penrith is a fine town – hundreds of people live there, and, that day being market-day, there must have been thousands pouring up the narrow streets, under the over-hanging houses. I wondered where on earth so many people would put themselves, not to mention their cattle and sheep, their riding-horses and pack-horses, their wagons and all. But when I got on into the centre of the town, the narrow streets broadened out suddenly into big squares, as a river broadens into a lake, and there was space for everyone. Penrith was planned like that, because of the Scots. When war came, the people drove all their flocks and herds into the middle, and by barricading the narrow streets turned the whole town into a fortress.

No one was thinking of danger that day; even I forgot

my trouble for a while when I saw all the cheerful bustle around me.

There weren't only the farmers parading their stock and the women laying out their eggs and butter and homespun cloth. All sorts of exciting strangers had come to the market – a swarthy man without any ears, leading a bear on a chain, a sword-swallower, a man who drew out your aching teeth (while your friends held you down), a couple of acrobats, and dozens of others doing strange tricks or selling miraculous remedies. One man was bellowing that there would be a great bull-baiting in the ring at noon, and inviting every man to bring his dog for the sport. I was listening to him when someone touched my shoulder and spoke, and I nearly jumped out of my skin.

'Hullo, Peter!'

It was only Tam Burney of Mungrisdale, but he gave me a start, for I'd never expected to see anyone I knew. Our folks all used Keswick Market.

I could see the old man knew everything that mattered. His frosty eyes twinkled. He laid a swollen forefinger to his bearded mouth.

'Whist, Peter boy, I'll say nothing! But' – he chuckled – 'that was a bad shot o' yours with the stone! Why didn't ye hit him, eh? There's plenty would have danced on his funeral day.'

'He was going pretty fast,' I said apologetically.

Tam looked more serious. 'You'll do well to get right out of the district, Peter boy. Sir Philip was like a madman yesterday, they say. Not for your stone, but for his beautiful wall. He's vowing Hell's vengeance on all who had a hand in it; but you're the only one, seemingly, he can prove anything against. I wouldn't be in your shoes, Peter boy.'

'I'm going away for a bit,' I admitted.

'That's right. Sir Philip's got too many friends among the magistrates. You'll not stand a dog's chance if they catch you. Where did you think of going?'

'Scotland, perhaps . . .'

Tam shook his head dubiously. 'They're expecting that. They've sent word to Carlisle to look out for you – that I know for a fact.'

'I could go cross-country and avoid Carlisle.'

'Too many big rivers to cross. I was up there twenty years back. You'll have to use the fords or the bridges, and that means you'll be noticed and talked-of – a young boy alone.'

'I'll manage,' I said; 'if need be, I'll swim.'

'Now don't try that on – might as well be hanged as drowned.'

That annoyed me, because I can swim as well as anyone. Some people think, because I'm not very big, that I'm not strong. I've swum miles in Derwentwater in my time.

'I'll be all right, Mr Burney,' I said. 'I don't think I'd better tell you my plans, had I? Then, if anyone asks you, you won't have to tell them any lies, will you?' And with that I said good morning, all very dignified, and walked off. I didn't like to admit that I still *hadn't* any plans. I began to look around the market in the hopes of finding some travelling merchant who wanted a handy boy to help with his packhorses. I thought I'd get out of Penrith more easily if I mixed myself up with a party, instead of travelling alone.

It wasn't so easy. I asked one man, and he snapped my head off. I asked another. No luck. The third man said more kindly:

'No; and if I wanted a boy I could have made my pick of dozens, every day I've travelled along the road. The country's crawling with them, all looking for work that isn't there. Take my advice, lad, and go back home.'

'I can't,' I said; 'I'm an orphan.'

'They're all orphans,' answered the merchant, and I could see he hadn't believed me. He turned away to sell a roll of green Kendal cloth to a parson's wife.

Outside one of the big inns there was a fat man wearing an old-fashioned helmet and beating a little drum that made everyone laugh: it looked so silly bobbing there against his immense belly. He stopped beating it after a moment, and looked round with a good-natured grin and began to speak. He had a wonderful voice, clear as a bell, and you could hear every word, even above the bleating of sheep, the shouting of the cheapjacks, and all the other hundred noises of market-day.

The famous London play-actors were here, he said, about to act one of the finest plays every written – the tragical history of *King Richard the Third*. They were doing it out of special compliment to the good people of Penrith – hadn't the wicked hunch-back usurper once lived in a house yonder, within a stone's throw of this spot; nay, within a strong man's spit? Wouldn't Penrith people like to see Richard again, as large as life, played by a London actor who had performed before Queen Elizabeth, supported by a full London company with drums, trumpets, and everything proper, regardless of expense? Admission one penny; stools to sit on, a penny extra. Starting now, in the inn-yard.

I was one of the first to pay my penny.

I wanted something to take my mind off homesick-ness and the fear of death or prison. So in I went – yes, and paid another penny for a stool to rest my weary bones, and yet another penny (reckless extravagance!) for a portion of hot roast mutton on a skewer. Wasn't it good to taste cooked food again!

By now the inn-yard was fairly crowded, and there were people filling the upper galleries all round, which led to the bedrooms. The players had rigged up a platform on trestles at one end of the yard, and we all moved round, some of us with our stools, but most of the people standing. I'd finished my mutton and licked my greasy fingers when suddenly I got a shock which turned the good food over inside me.

Sir Philip Morton was coming through the archway into the yard.

He paused to give his penny to the man, and I saw his lean face sideways, with the little golden beard springing from the cruel under-lip, and the blue eyes so cold and insolent.

'And we'll have stools, my man, on the stage. What? No stools allowed on the stage? Absurd! Too poky, I suppose. Very well.' He turned and waved a gloved hand towards my corner of the yard. 'Put me two over there, then.'

I thought I was done for.

There was only the one archway leading from the yard, and Sir Philip stood there, ordering wine. I could not pass him, but if I stayed where I was he would come and sit down almost beside me.

I looked round like a fox trapped on a ledge. Then I thought of the galleries.

A staircase rose close behind me. If I went up there I might find some other way out, or at any rate I might be able to lie hidden in some room till the play was over.

Without wasting any more time, I slipped off my stool and up that staircase. The gallery was already crowded with people, ready settled to see the play. One way they were so thickly packed that I couldn't push quickly through without starting an uproar, which was the last thing I wanted to do. The other way there weren't so many. Just then I heard Sir Philip's voice on the stairs:

'We should see better up here, Roger, and we shouldn't get our toes trodden on by these clodhopping shepherds.'

'Just as you like, Phil.'

I didn't wait for more. There was a curtained doorway at the end of the gallery, and I made for it, stumbling over people's heels and mumbling my apologies.

'Hey! you there, *boy*!'

That was Sir Philip's voice from the top of the stairs. He'd seen me. I rushed on, flung out my hand to part the curtain.

'Stop that boy!' he shouted.

I heard the people behind me cursing heartily at being disturbed when the play was about to begin. I hurled myself through the curtain, round the corner of a dark landing, and down a staircase. I found myself in the midst of a crowd of feverishly excited people – I was in the actors' dressing-room.

A boy was being helped into an immense hooped skirt, the fat man was grumbling because his armour would not meet round the back, a tall, gloomy young man was reciting lines to himself in a thin, birdlike voice . . . This much I had time to take in before the fat man bellowed at me:

'Who are you? What do you want? Get out of here! We're ready to go on, and I *will* not have outsiders behind the scene. Vanish, before I rend you limb from limb!'

He was a terrifying figure. I ducked under his arm, getting no more than a glancing clout which made my head sing, and rushed round a corner into another passage. Behind me I heard him roaring:

'What? More intruders! Out with you, sir! I don't care if you're Sir –'

'This gentleman with me is a magistrate,' Sir Philip cut in very icily.

I heard this all plainly, for the very good reason that I was trapped in the passage outside. There were only two doors leading from it, and they were both locked. The passage seemed to be a dumping-ground for stage properties and costumes.

I thought wildly for a moment of disguising myself in one of these costumes – a woman's spreading skirts would have been the best concealment – but I realized that the actors would give me away at once.

'My friend is a magistrate,' Sir Philip was saying, 'and you'll realize that, if he likes, he can forbid your play altogether and ruin your tour in this part of the country. So you'd better be civil.'

'What do you want, sir?' the fat man growled. I could tell he was bottling up his fury with great difficulty.

You mustn't think that I stood still, listening to their talk and doing nothing. The whole thing took only a few seconds, and I wasted none of them.

There was a big chest among the actors' properties; I suppose it was used for storing costumes when they moved from place to place. It was long, narrow, and deep. Also, it was empty and unlocked.

It was a desperate chance, but the only one. I hopped inside and pulled down the lid. As I did so I heard a trumpet sound, and a great burst of stamping and clapping in the distance. The fat man's voice sounded despairing:

'But, gentlemen, the play's just beginning!'

'Carry on with your play; we don't mind,' said Sir Philip. 'But we insist on searching these rooms.'

4.

There is Safety in Coffins

I could hear the voice of the fat man, farther away now and muffled by the box:

> *'Now is the winter of our discontent*
> *Made glorious summer by this sun of York . . .'*

and I knew that he had gone away to take his place on the stage. There was a great hushing and shushing from the actors, and they all began to go about on tiptoe and speak in whispers. But I could distinctly hear Sir Philip and his friend questioning people and opening doors.

Would they come and examine the chest? I lay there in a hot sweat, my heart thumping away like a water-wheel. After a little while I heard the man Roger say:

'I've asked the inn people, and they swear no one's gone out from here.'

'And the actors say they saw him, but the idiots didn't notice where he went to! Never mind. We'll find him.'

Sir Philip sounded ready to spend the whole afternoon on his search. I heard footsteps approaching. Someone said:

'Where's that coffin, Bob?'

'In there. Come on.'

The footsteps stopped beside me. I almost stopped breathing. There was a grunt from Bob, whoever he was, and I felt myself swung in the air, then put down again on something that creaked.

'It's mighty heavy,' Bob grumbled. 'Suppose there isn't a *real* body inside it?'

'Course not. It's *supposed* to be empty.'

'That it isn't, anyway. They must have left some of the props inside, 'stead of unpacking properly. Let's throw 'em out –'

'No, there's no time; we're wanted on the stage. Quick! sling that velvet cloth over it. Now the crown on the top – remember, it's s'posed to be Henry the Sixth inside! You take the front. Ready? Off we go.'

Again I felt myself lifted into the air, and this time I stayed there – or rather I moved rapidly forward, head first inside the chest.

'Mind your back, sir!' said Bob hoarsely, and I heard

Sir Philip swear under his breath; I imagine someone had trodden on his toe.

The next moment I heard a high, squeaky voice reciting:

> *'Set down, set down your honourable load –*
> *If honour may be shrouded in a hearse –'*

and I knew, as I was set down on a creaking floor, that we had reached the public stage. That was my first theatrical appearance – if you can call it an appearance when you are lying in a wooden chest under a black velvet pall – and I can't say I enjoyed it.

There was a long, long speech by the squeaky voice, which was supposed to be that of the Lady Anne Some-body, but which all too clearly belonged to a boy whose voice was just breaking, for every now and again he stopped squeaking and growled like a bear for the rest of the sentence, so that some of the audience laughed when they should have been moved to tears.

At the end of this speech the men picked me up again, and for a few moments I was scared lest they should carry me off the stage, back into the danger zone; but to my relief I heard the fat man cry out in his juicy voice:

'Stay, you that bear the corse, and set it down!'

and after a few lines of furious argument, all in verse, set it down they did, and I knew I was safe for a little longer.

It proved to be a long scene, and in my normal circumstances I should have been fidgeting, because the boy taking the Lady Anne's part was terrible. But as it was, knowing what was waiting for me behind the scenes, I wanted it to go on for hours. All too soon the Lady Anne swept off the stage, with only that sort of clapping that one gives out of kindness and charity, and a few lines later I followed her in my coffin.

'What *have* they left in this box?' grumbled the man named Bob, as they set me down with a bump behind the scenes. I heard his hand fumbling with the catch of the lid, but once more his companion saved me.

'Don't waste time, man; we're on in the next scene as the Murderers. We've got to look sharp and change.'

'All right, all right! What a play for a touring company! Six parts apiece, and changing your clothes as often as the Queen herself!'

There was a brief silence then, during which I could hear the actors on the stage. I strained my ears, but I couldn't detect a hint of Sir Philip's presence. Had he gone? I was glad when the man Bob settled the question by calling softly to one of his friends:

'Where's Lord High-an'-Mighty?'

'Oh, he cleared of – after turning everything upside-down. It's a wonder he didn't want to slit the linings of our doublets and look for the boy there.'

'What's he want with the boy?'

'Attempted murder. Heaved a rock at His Lord-ship.'

'Don't blame him. Hope he gets away all right.'

'He won't do that. His Lordship said he was going to comb the town for him, and set a watch on all the roads leading out of it.'

'I see. Poor little devil hasn't a chance.'

'Not a hope.'

A new voice cut in then, calm and matter-of-fact: 'First and Second Murderers – ready?'

'Ay, ay,' said Bob, and off they went to take their cue. Murderers or monks or mourners, it was all the same to them, just a part to play. I envied them.

It was hot in the chest, but I was afraid to come out. I could never be sure, even when there was silence around me, that there wasn't at least one actor in the room. I think I would have risked it in the case of Bob, who sounded kindly and would not, perhaps, have given me away. But the others I daren't trust. So I stayed in my stifling box for the present, hoping that some means of escape would present itself eventually.

All through that hot summer's afternoon the long drama of *Richard the Third* unfolded itself. The trumpets sang, the drums beat, and, when there was supposed to be a battle raging off-stage, all the actors who had nothing better to do danced madly round me, yelling, stamping, and beating swords together, to sound like an army of thousands. My head ached as though it would crack. Resting as it did on the hard wood, it felt every vibration from the floor. I was nearly dead from suffocation and lack of sleep, but the row kept me fully conscious.

So Sir Philip was combing the town for me. Was going to set a watch on each of the roads leading out of it. The situation was desperate, but with each narrow escape I was getting more and more weary of the whole business. I just wanted this wild adventure to end, even if it ended in capture.

The play ended. I heard the applause of the audience, their babbling murmur as they dispersed, and the eager chatter of the players all round me. Some were discussing the takings; they sounded pleased when they heard that the doorman had collected nearly forty shillings. Others talked in lower tones, gossip and grumbles mainly – how William Desmond was too fat now to play Richard, and how bad 'Lady Anne' was, and how somebody else was never given a proper-sized part.

That sort of talk stopped suddenly when (as I guessed) the leading man came bustling in.

'Look alive, lads!' he said. 'Get your things off, and pack up; the wagons are waiting. It's twenty-five miles or more to Kendal, and you know what the roads are like in this country. It'll be dark before we get there as it is.'

Kendal! A gleam of hope cut the darkness of my despair. So the actors were going straight on to Kendal that very evening? If only I could remain hidden they would carry me right through Sir Philip's cordon . . . Carlisle would have been better, perhaps, but Kendal would do well enough. If I wasn't discovered . . .

That was too much to hope. But, perhaps, if I threw myself on their mercy, they wouldn't give me away? Sir Philip hadn't made himself popular by bursting in upon them during the play. They wouldn't be particularly anxious to do him a good turn.

On the other hand, I reminded myself, these touring actors went in mortal fear of the magistrates. They had to get permission before they could set up their stage in any town, and if they were found to be helping a criminal – it was queer to think of myself as that! – they might be put out of business. Also, there might be at least one among so poverty-stricken a crew who would jump at the chance to earn a reward by betraying me to Sir Philip.

No. I wasn't going to trust these actors unless I was compelled to.

They were packing now. Boxes were bumped about, men were accusing each other of borrowing and mislaying their property, and the two or three boys in the company were being chivvied around by everyone. In the middle of it all the innkeeper's wife stormed in and made a fearful to-do about a quart of ale which had been sent in but never paid for. Now the actors had changed their costumes she could not recognize the man who had ordered it, and no one would own up. I never knew how it ended. I heard a boy ask:

'Where do these go, Mrs Desmond?'

A comfortable, motherly voice answered: 'Oh, where there's room for 'em dearie. Usually I put 'em in that big box we use as the coffin.'

Now for it! My heart bounded sickeningly.

'That box is about full, if you ask me,' Bob's voice broke in. 'Never been unpacked. Ben and I noticed how heavy it was when –'

'If it's ready to go,' interrupted the fat man impatiently, 'for goodness' sake put it on the wagon. We're late.'

'Very well, Mr Desmond.'

Once again I felt myself swung off the ground. They carried me out into the yard; their footfalls changed suddenly from the hollowness of wooden floors to the ring of cobbles. I had an unpleasant moment or two when they tilted the chest sharply to put it on the wagon, for the top end happened to be the one where my feet were, so I was jerked back head downwards, giving my skull a nasty tap and my neck a jolt which almost dislocated it.

Still, it was worth it. It was a step nearer safety. With luck, I reckoned, I should soon be out of the zone of particular danger. I would wait till Penrith was well behind us; then, some time before we reached Kendal, I would seize my chance to come out of my stuffy tomb. I should be seen, no doubt, but I reckoned on the surprise dumbfounding them all. It would be the work of a moment to pop out of the chest, jump from the tail of the wagon, and dash into the moor beside the road. It would be twilight by then, and if any London actor could catch me in my own country, I should be interested to meet him.

The first part of my plan went excellently.

After an age, the last bundle was heaved into the wagon, and half a dozen of the players scrambled in. The driver chirruped and away we lumbered under the archway, down the street, and out of town.

We weren't stopped at all. I heard the driver shout to someone: 'Found him yet?' but the answer was lost to me in the rumble of wheels. 'What you want,' said the driver, 'is a bloodhound.' He drove on without slackening speed.

The actors chattered like magpies for the first mile or two. Then someone began passing round a quart pot of ale, and after that it was singing, one song after another.

In spite of the bumping, I dropped off to sleep. My last memory was of all the actors singing:

> *'Come, Night, and lay thy velvet hand*
> *On glorious Day's outfacing face . . .*

Away rumbled our wagons down the winding road between the twilit fells, and Night laid her velvet hand on my face so that I slept like one of the dead. The second half of my plan was never fulfilled.

5.

Someone Was Watching

We never got to Kendal that night.

We took a wrong turning in the dark, and wasted an hour getting back to the proper road. A wheel came off the other wagon, and, as it was in front and the road just there very narrow, we all had to wait till the damage was repaired. Finally, as it was a warm night, the company decided to camp where they were till daylight, thus saving the expense at the inn. They would still arrive at Kendal in good time for the afternoon performance.

I knew nothing of this till afterwards. I woke to hear a great discussion going on near by. I realized at once that the wagon had stopped.

'Don't be a fool, William,' the motherly woman was saying.

'I tell you there's something inside, Jane!' The fat man sounded pathetic, like a frightened child.

'Of course there's something inside –'

'Something that moved and made a noise!'

'It's that play that's got on your mind. I always said there were too many ghosts in *Richard the Third* –'

'Listen, Jane! Now, that isn't fancy!'

I couldn't stand the chest any longer; luckily, it was a roughly made thing of boards bounded with iron, and some air got through the cracks, otherwise I should have been suffocated hours before. I tried now to push open the lid, but I was so cramped and weak that I could hardly move it.

Suddenly the lid lifted, there was a gasp of amazement, and there in the yellow lantern light was a plump woman's face hanging over me like a harvest moon.

'Well, I'll be hanged! Come here, William, and see what the fairies have left us!'

Without waiting for her husband, she slipped a massive arm under my shoulders and raised me till I was sitting up like a sick baby in its cot.

'Don't stand gaping, all of you,' she shouted over her shoulder as the others came clustering round. 'Get me some of that water, quick, and a bowl of stew. And, William, just a thimbleful of that wine, if you can spare it.'

In five minutes, sitting beside a cheerful fire on the grass, I was myself again. I started to stammer explanations and apologies, but William Desmond cut me short with a grand gesture.

'Not a word, boy, not a word! Least said soonest mended. We met you on the Kendal road. We cannot remember ever having seen you before. You have an honest look. It naturally does not occur to us to associate you with the youthful criminal of Penrith. No one can ever accuse my company of knowingly harbouring a fugitive from justice.'

'They can accuse us,' interjected his wife bluntly, 'but they can't prove it.'

So I turned to my supper again and cleaned up a second bowl of excellent stew. I was still terribly tired, but I had a wonderful feeling of relief. They were all so kind, not only Mr and Mrs Desmond, but the others sitting round the fire. I felt I had reached safety.

I looked round at the scene, over the rim of my bowl. I didn't know quite where we were, for I had never travelled so far from home. But the moonlight showed me low ridges of moor on either side of the road, with a hint of higher fells to the westward. Our wagons were drawn up in a dip, where a beck came rippling across the road. The horses were tethered a few paces away, finding what feed they could among the rough moor grasses.

Safety? It seemed so, in that warm circle of fire-glow. But I couldn't help wondering.

When you are used to being alone on the fells, I think you get very sensitive to the presence of other people. You feel it particularly when you are being watched.

I got a queer feeling as I sat by the fire that *we* were being watched.

I don't mean that just I was, but the whole troupe. Of course, the actors were watching me as I finished my supper, and I expect they were wondering all sorts of things about me. But I don't count the straightforward look of a friendly stranger who has just met you.

No, it was as though someone was watching us secretly, from outside the circle of the fire. Someone crouching in the tall, dew-wet bracken, watching with two bright eyes that fairly bored the darkness.

It was a queer fancy, but there was nothing I could do about it. You could have hidden an army in those rustling acres of bracken, so there was little enough chance of finding one man. I shivered – but that was only the chilliness which comes with lack of sleep. William Desmond suddenly burst out, after studying me in silence for a couple of minutes:

'Can you sing, boy?'

I started. I felt quite unlike singing just then, but I was prepared to do my best if required to earn my supper.

'Tomorrow,' he explained rapidly, 'we are doing *The*

Two Gentlemen of Verona. There is a song, an exquisite song. We always have it sung by a page-boy. But have we a page-boy in the company who can sing a note?' He looked round at them all defiantly, but no one spoke. 'George's voice is like a broken pot. Young Francis, who could sing like an angel, ran away and left us at Lancaster – frightened, miserable little puppy, of these mountains! We're left so short-handed there's scarcely a play we can put on if it has more than two female characters in it.' He turned to me again. 'Could you learn this song and sing it for us? Nothing else to do at all.'

> *'Who is Silvia? What is she,*
> *That all our swains commend her?'*

It seemed an easy song, with only three short verses. I promised to do my best. I was glad to make some return, even if it was so small, for the kindness the actors had shown me.

The important thing now was to get some sleep, so I curled myself up on a great roll of tapestry in the wagon and went off so soundly that I never woke when they harnessed the horses at dawn and moved on again.

When I did open my eyes the sun was up and the morning was full of bird-calls. I raised myself on my elbow and looked over the wagon-side.

We were still moving between ridges of moorland, but I guessed we were not far from our destination. I could see the broad backs of Mr and Mrs Desmond – he was driving that wagon – but most of the company were walking along in twos and threes.

'Hi!'

There were black figures suddenly on the shaggy grass skyline to the left, men waving their arms, horses with manes and tails streaming darkly against the dazzling gold of the morning.

'Hi, there! *Stop!*'

The cry came thinly down, as cries do in mountain air.

There were four men, I could see, as I peeped cautiously over the wagon-side.

'Drive on,' said Mrs Desmond to her husband, very tensely. The wagon had never stopped, anyhow. We rumbled on.

'I'll drop off,' I began, 'and run up the other –'

'You'll do nothing of the sort,' she said, without turning her head. 'Lie where you are, pull some things over you, and don't make a sound.' I did as she told me; there was no arguing with Mrs Desmond, as I was beginning to learn. I couldn't get into my coffin again because it was in the other wagon, but I hid myself as best I could among the other baggage. My last glimpse of the horsemen showed them galloping aslant the hill, to cut us off at the next bend. We hadn't a dog's chance of outdistancing them.

Sure enough, it was barely two minutes before I heard the clatter of hooves in front and the whine of our wheels as we came to a standstill.

'What's this?' Desmond shouted in his lordliest tone. 'We're overdue in Kendal as it is. What do you mean by . . .' His voice faded. He had jumped down from the driving-seat and walked up the road. I could hear the voices of the strangers, but I couldn't make out a word. Then I heard footsteps coming back. Desmond was grumbling.

'My dear sir, I assure you –'

'I should prefer to have a look, all the same.'

'Do you doubt my word, sir?' stormed the actor.

'Not at all, not at all. But the back of your wagon is open; someone might have crept in without your knowing.'

I wished I had run for it. It was too late now. I knew that in a stand-up fight my new friends would have been more than a match for the four strangers, but it would have been unfair to let it come to that. I could not let them all go to jail for me, and that was what it would mean in the long run, since no jury would believe the word of vagabond actors against that of the local gentry. If they discovered me now – and only a miracle could prevent it – I would swear that I had hidden myself in the wagon without anyone's knowledge.

'Very well,' said Desmond suddenly, as if weary of the argument. 'Look, if you want to.'

I don't know what else he could have done, but I must admit that I felt a pang of disappointment in him. I heard a man spring on to the tail of the wagon.

'There *is* someone hiding here!' he burst out in triumph, and instantly dragged me out; even I was taken aback by the suddenness with which his hand fell on my shoulder.

'But it's only a boy!' said an older man, looking at me with disgust.

'Of course,' said Mrs Desmond without a second's hesitation.'It's that idle young scallywag, Sammy. Always hiding and going to sleep to dodge the work!'

'Hop out, you little devil!' her husband ordered me. 'Do a little walking for a change.'

I hopped out obediently, and the four strangers never gave me another glance. They went along to the other wagon, but of course they found no one there. They remounted, and I must say they apologized for the trouble they had given us before cantering off along the road again. Desmond called after them:

'If we *do* see the lady we'll send word to the Hall.'

'What was all that about?' I asked eagerly as I swung myself into the wagon again.

The actor laughed. 'They were searching for a young lady. She ran away from home during the night – some family trouble, I expect, though, of course, they weren't letting us into their private affairs.'

'Eloped, probably,' said his wife sentimentally. She had seen so many romantic Italian comedies, had Jane Desmond, that she could never think of love without going as sloppy as porridge. It was the only thing wrong with her, to my mind; she was a kindly, great-hearted woman, and after knowing her a week or two I would have fought to the death for her as I would have done for my own mother.

I didn't worry my head about the incident any more. We were coming down from the hills now, and Kendal lay below us in the rich green bowl of the valley. In an hour or two I should be making a real appearance on the public stage. I ran through my song several times to make sure I had it by heart.

We set up our stage in the yard of an inn. It was a poor pitch compared with the one at Penrith, and the inn rooms were so inconveniently placed that most of us had to dress in the wagons. Mrs Desmond told me I could sleep in the wagon that night if I liked, and I accepted gratefully. My future was still uncertain, and I was glad to save the cost of a night's lodging.

Well, there isn't much to tell about the rest of that day. Nothing out of the ordinary happened. I didn't have stage-fright or anything funny. I walked on with the others when they told me, wearing a vivid yellow doublet which was rather tight across the shoulders, and when the music started I sang my song. People clapped – not a lot, but enough to make me feel quite pleased, and Mrs Desmond gave me a great slap on the back when I came off. My doublet thereupon split with a swishing noise, and she cursed like a carter, but quite cheerfully, as she rummaged for needle and thread.

'Lucky you haven't to go on again,' she said, pricking me between the shoulder-blades. 'What do you think of the play?'

'Very nice,' I said politely.

'I'm glad young Shakespeare's turning to comedy instead of those noisy histories with a battle every ten minutes and an execution or two between to keep up the interest. There's enough of that in real life, I say, so give the public something light like *The Two Gentlemen*. As for tragedy, they might as well stop trying to write it, now poor Kit Marlowe's gone . . .'

'Who was he?'

'The best of the bunch! You should see his *Doctor Faustus* – we still do it sometimes, you know. Or his *Jew of Malta*. The plays he wrote! He was no older than this young man from Warwickshire, but what's Shakespeare done or likely to do compared with him?'

'What happened to Mr Marlowe?' I asked.

'Stabbed to death,' she answered, with a sigh. 'We never heard the whole truth of it, and I doubt if we ever shall. But, there . . . Let's change the subject. You've a nice voice, Peter. Weren't you nervous at the thought of all the people watching you?'

'Oh no,' I said, and it was true. I hadn't minded about the people in the yard. Only once, as I sang the last verse, I'd suddenly felt that same queer feeling of someone watching me – not the frank, open stare of the crowd, but the intense gaze of someone watching from a hidden place.

Of course, that was all so fanciful that I couldn't possibly explain it to her, so I said nothing. I soon forgot all about it.

We had a jolly evening after the performance, for the actors, having saved their night's lodging by camping on the road, were determined to make up for it and spend the money on a better supper than usual. They all congratulated me on my tiny part in the show, and Desmond said:

'Why not stay with us for a bit, Peter? It'll only be for a month or two; we're working our way back to London before the winter sets in. Then goodness knows what'll happen to us all, but who's worrying now?'

Who's worrying now? Not a bad motto, I thought to myself. I accepted the offer. As I fell asleep that night on my bed of baggage, I murmured happily: 'I'm going to London; I've got work; I'm an actor!'

It was an exciting thought, but no amount of excitement would have kept me awake that night. I slept soundly till nearly dawn, when, I suppose, some noise startled me, for I sat bolt upright, blinking round in the grey light.

I knew at once that I was no longer alone in the wagon. If I had doubted that for a moment, the doubt would soon have been settled. Before I could even turn my head a voice spoke softly but emphatically in my right ear:

'If you make a sound, I'll stick this knife in your gizzard!'

6.

Rivals on the Road

You know that awful feeling when your heart seems to jump, and stop – as though it were hanging in the air mid-way between its proper place and the ceiling? That's how I felt.

'Promise you won't yell?' said the voice again. I could tell now that it was a boy's voice, young, but deep and musical. There was something in its tone which suggested that my gizzard wasn't really in such great danger.

'All right,' I grunted, twisting round on my elbow.

The boy was kneeling behind me, and sure enough he had a small dagger which made a streak of white light in the gloom. I could see that he was small too, and perhaps a year or two younger than myself. I felt secretly ashamed of my fear.

'What are *you* doing here, my lad?' I said roughly, remembering that I was now a member of the company and in charge of their baggage.

'The same as you,' he retorted cheekily. 'Getting some sleep.'

'But *I'm* one of the actors.'

'Since when?'

I could have knocked his block off – cheerfully – for that, but it wouldn't have been fair. I told him to mind his own business. He just smiled, looking me up and down as though I were something on four legs, with a tail, in Keswick Market.

'I think I'll become an actor,' he said lazily.

'Huh!' I snorted. 'It's not so easy.'

'It can't be so *very* difficult . . . if *you* are.'

I asked him if he was looking for a thick ear. He said, No; he was looking for work. I assured him he wasn't the only one; the roads of England were strung with beggars like beads on a thread. As for work as an actor . . . well, I didn't tell an outright lie, but I rather suggested that there were no vacancies in William Desmond's company.

Don't think that, in doing this, I was just playing dog-in-the-manger. I was scared of having another Cumberland boy in the company; I wanted to get right away from Cumberland for the present and break all links, otherwise the news of my whereabouts might filter back to Sir Philip Morton. Also, this boy had such colossal self-confidence that he would probably be a startling success and quite push me out of my present place in the sun.

He looked at me with that mocking, impish grin of his, and said drawlingly:

'My word, you *are* a little liar.'

I knew then that he had been the unseen watcher that night by the roadside. That he had been close to us ever since, creeping nearer and nearer, peeping at us from hiding-places . . . He must know considerably more about me than was healthy.

But I wasn't going to be called a liar by anyone, so I jumped up and swung my fist, but he ducked under my arm and leapt off the tail of the wagon. I followed. There was a pump in the yard, and I felt it would be a good idea to hold his head under it for a minute or two, before booting him out into the street. But I never did so, for William Desmond was bending under it himself, sluicing his red neck in the icy water – a thing I never saw any of the other actors do.

'What's this? What's this?' he demanded, straightening up and looking from one to the other of us.

'This little fool –' I started.

'– wants to join your company,' interrupted the boy, and dropped Desmond a curtsey that wouldn't have disgraced the Queen's waiting-women. I saw Desmond gape. Before he could speak, the boy added hurriedly: 'Tell *him* to try that; I bet he can't. He's like all the other boys in your company, Mr Desmond – dress 'em up as much as you like, they don't look like ladies, but boys in skirts.'

Desmond went redder than his towel had already made him. He turned to me: 'Try a curtsey, Peter.'

I tried, and failed – I'd never noticed how it was done. I tried again, sticking out one leg in front of me, and sinking down on the other heel. For a moment I rocked uncertainly, then I lost my balance and rolled over in a rather dirty patch of the yard. The way they laughed didn't improve my temper.

'It's just practice,' I said, 'and it would come easier when I was dressed up for it.'

'That's right,' said Desmond kindly, as if he was sorry he'd laughed. 'There's more in acting than dropping curtseys.'

'I should hope so,' the boy agreed immediately. His face changed suddenly to a most tragic expression, which, in my jealousy, I might have described as that of a dying duck in a thunderstorm. Only – luckily for me – I noticed in time that Desmond's eyes were alight with interest as the boy recited:

> *'Set down, set down, your honourable load –*
> *If honour may be shrouded in a hearse . . .'*

Then, after a few lines, he broke off, ceased to be a wailing widow, and changed to a kittenish maiden from some comedy or other.

'Stop!' said Desmond. 'Where did you learn to act, boy?'

The boy looked away. 'Does it matter, sir?'

'I suppose not . . . You've talent. We could use you. What's your name?'

'Kit – short for Christopher,' answered the boy.

'Kit what?'

'Kit Kirkstone,' he said without hesitating, but with something in his voice which told me he was lying. I said so. I was still angry because he had called me a liar, and all the angrier because he had been right.

'He's making that up,' I interrupted. 'Kirkstone isn't a surname; it's the name of a pass between the mountains, over to Patterdale.'

The boy looked at me, his blue eyes flashing with fury and his little nose wrinkling up with contempt. Then he swung round on the actor with a charming smile.

'All the more reason why my name should . . . *pass*!'

It was a poor sort of pun, but in those days we thought a lot of puns: they were the favourite form of humour, and no playwright could have written a page without them. Desmond laughed.

'The boy's got wit, too!'

'Kit the Wit,' I muttered.

Desmond gave me a glance which silenced me. 'Kirkstone will pass,' he chuckled. 'We ask no awkward questions here. The present is what matters, not the past. You two boys must be friends; we are all friends in this company.'

I put my hand out at that, and Kit took it. I gripped his till I saw the tears start in his eyes, but I stopped before hurting him as much as I should have liked to do. It seemed suddenly rather mean and cowardly, for he was inches shorter than I, and although he might, like me, be stronger and tougher than he looked, I felt pretty sure he wasn't. There was something just a bit soft and girlish about him, and I suppose it was that, along with his impudence, which put me off.

But he could act! Give the devil his due. He *could* act!

We had no performance to give that day, but we were busy from morning till night. *The Two Gentlemen of Verona* was to be acted again in two days' time, when our southward journey had brought us to Lancaster. Kit was set to learn the part of Julia, the heroine who leaves home disguised as a man, to find her lover. I was to be Lucetta, her maid.

When I remember all the other pieces I acted in afterwards, I realize what light, thin stuff *The Two Gentlemen* was. The plot was just the usual mixture that I saw served up in the theatre, time and time again, in play after play. Oh, those disguised heroines! How sick we got of playing them! Of course, there was a reason why the author always fell back on the old trick. We boys had to take all the women's parts, and it was hard to make us look right. It was easy, in a way, to step out of our hooped skirts and farthingales into the tight hose we wore in ordinary life – and then pretend to pretend what we really were. That sounds complicated, but you know what I mean.

Kit Kirkstone didn't need any help of that kind.

He was the only one of us all – and there were three other boys, old stagers, in the company – who really looked like a woman when he was dressed for the part. He had everything – the walk, the head-tossing, the eye-play, the hand movements . . . all the gestures which I had to be taught, slowly and patiently, because I had never observed them in real life from the women around me.

Desmond corrected him once on some small point; I forget even what it was, and I fancy he did it more to prevent the boy from getting any more conceited than he must have been already.

'No, no!' said the actor suddenly. 'Not like that – no woman in the world ever did it that way.'

Kit turned on him, scarlet-faced, hands on hips. 'I know perfectly well how to do it!' he retorted.

That wasn't the way to talk to Desmond. He heaved his great bulk out of his chair and towered above Kit terrifyingly.

'You contradict *me*?' he boomed. 'I – who have been twenty years in the London theatre? How should *you* know better, you – you farthing?'

'I – I'm sorry, sir,' Kit apologized, cooling and dropping his eyes. 'Only I – you see, I have five sisters at home, and I've studied them, and imitated them . . . I was so set on going to London and being an actor . . . and I knew this was the best way for a boy to start, and . . .'

He stopped, as if he had already told us too much. I wondered how much was true. It was quite likely he had run away from home to join the company, and that would account for his rather mysterious behaviour. Plenty of decent people did disapprove of the stage even then, and it was more than probable that if Kit's father knew where he was, Kit would be hauled home and given a warm greeting where he did not want it.

He was a strange lad. His clothes were poor and fitted badly. I don't think, when he joined us, he had a penny in his pocket. Yet, when he made some notes on the margin of his play-script, he wrote a hand that would have rejoiced my master at Keswick. He had the speech and manners of a gentleman.

He would talk freely about some things, such as the books he had read, but not a word of himself, his family, school, or where he lived. From one remark he let out, I guessed he had been to London once before, but as soon as I asked a question he became as dumb and stubborn as an old ram. That night he slept on the other side of the wagon from me. I began to suspect that he was not only a little beast, but a dirty little beast as well, for I never saw him wash the next morning. He *said* he had got up early and washed before anyone else was awake, but that is a tale I have heard often – and told myself more than once in cold weather.

We were starting for Lancaster in an hour or two. Mrs Desmond poked her motherly head into the wagon.

'I don't want to meddle in anyone's business,' she said, 'but there's a man starting north who says he'll carry letters anywhere within reason; he's going all round, peddling his goods, and he's honest, for we've met him before. If you boys care to write a line to your people, just to tell them you're all right . . .'

'Thank you, Mrs Desmond,' I said, and Kit said, Yes, he'd write too.

So we got ink and pens and paper quickly, and wrote, lying on our stomachs in the wagon. I worded my letter carefully, lest it should fall into wrong hands. On Mrs Desmond's suggestion, I told them they could write back to me, care of her, at the Flower de Luce Tavern in Southwark. Then, when it was safe for me to go home, they could send word.

Kit wrote quickly, as if he were an author and his living depended on his speed with the pen. By the time I had written my one letter, he had finished two. We went together and got them sealed.

'Shall I take them to the man?' I offered, hoping to read the addresses.

'No, thanks, I'll go. Shall I take yours?'

I wasn't having that. I was Peter Brown to the company, but the letter was addressed to Mrs Brownrigg, and I wasn't going to risk his seeing it.

'Don't be standoffish,' I said. 'You needn't think I'm inquisitive.'

More to annoy him than anything, I snatched his letters and started to walk away. But I had gone only a pace or two before he was on me like a tiger-cat, ripping them from my grasp, and streaking round the corner before I could catch him.

I had held them in my hand only a moment, but there had been time to read the address on the one uppermost. It was directed to *'Sir Philip Morton, Lonsdale Hall, near Keswick.'*

7.

Who is Kit Kirkstone?

Who was Kit Kirkstone? Why was he writing to the only real enemy I had in the world?

The questions racked my brain for the next few days and prevented my enjoying what would otherwise have been a wholly delightful experience – the slow, halting journey from one strange town to another, the happy-go-lucky company of the actors, and the adventure of strutting before an audience in scarlet and yellow and lilac finery, bright enough for the Court itself.

Kit Kirkstone spoilt it for me. The others said I was prejudiced against him, but surely I had reason?

I couldn't imagine what game he was playing. If he knew all about me, why didn't he go straight to the first magistrate and denounce me? That wouldn't have been difficult. In each town where we played we had first to secure a signed permit from two Justices of the Peace. It happened sometimes that one of us boys went with Desmond to call at their houses. Kit had every chance to see magistrates if he wanted to.

But nothing happened, and, after we had passed through half a dozen towns, I gave up wondering when the constable's hand would fall on my shoulder. Kit showed no special interest in me – or in anyone else for that matter, for he lived a strange aloof existence, with his nose buried in any book he could lay hands on. The other boys, Tom and Dennis and Harry, tried to get him to join in our games; we had quite a lot of fun between whiles, what with football, wrestling, and swimming. Kit wouldn't join our swimming parties even on the hottest day, and I guessed it was because he couldn't swim and was afraid. He flared up at that in a moment:

'I can swim the width of Ullswater, anyhow!'

Even at the narrowest part of the lake, I reckon that would be a good quarter of a mile, so I told him I'd believe it when I saw him do it. He just shrugged his shoulders and walked off in a huff. After that, the other boys sided with me. They weren't too pleased, anyhow, at an outsider like him walking straight into the best parts, though Harry didn't mind much now his voice had broken and he was tall enough to play male characters.

Well, as I say, Kit Kirkstone showed no interest in

me. I imagine he had sent news of me to Sir Philip, and was leaving the rest to him. If he cared to send after me – and if his messenger could ever catch up with the zigzag wanderings of our company – no doubt there would be trouble in store for me. But at least Kit was making no trouble himself, so far as I could see.

I never saw him write another letter, though I kept my eyes open. If I saw another addressed to Sir Philip, I meant to read more than the name on the outside.

Meanwhile, as the weeks passed, there were other more pressing anxieties.

The farther I travelled from Cumberland, the less I worried about Sir Philip, and the more I began to share in the continual daily cares and disappointments of an actor's life.

It is a hard profession. That summer and autumn, as our wagons rumbled down the western side of England, we barely paid our way.

True, the towns got bigger as we went south, and the autumn fairs brought big crowds together. But the crowds were more critical – and a lot of us didn't act well enough to bear much criticism. It had been all right in Cumberland and Westmorland and the hill-towns of Lancashire, for Desmond was almost the first manager to lead a company into those regions, which Londoners thought of as savage, barbarous deserts on the fringe of the Arctic. But Chester hooted when they saw Richard the Third's army represented by two men and a boy, and Worcester hissed us off the stage when we gave them the good old comedy of *Ralph Roister-doister*, while at Stratford everyone went off to a cockfight, leaving us to play to an empty yard.

Sometimes, when a town had a strong Puritan flavour, we couldn't even get permission to act at all. At one place the parson preached an hour's sermon against us – I know, for we were there on the Sunday, and attended church to show what a decent, well-behaved crew we were.

It was no good. According to the preacher, we were responsible for all the evils which afflicted modern England.

'When Britons ate acorns and drank water,'he thundered, 'they were giants and heroes. Yet, since plays came in, they have dwindled to a puny race!'

Then he went on to explain that even the plague was our fault. Plays cause sin, he reasoned. Sin causes plagues. Therefore, plays cause plagues. That was the gist of his argument, though he wrapped it up in long words and texts.

When we struck a town like that, it meant no money to share out, it meant trying to sleep with no supper in your belly, and a night by the roadside instead of the comfort of an inn. Not that that made any difference to me; I always slept in the wagon, and so now did all the other boys. It saved a penny or two.

So we struggled on towards London, hoping that October would be fine and golden, not a month of flooded roads and fog.

But we were unlucky. The rain came – not rain as we know it in Cumberland, violent slashing rain like a charge of cavalry, giving way after a while to blue skies and vivid sun, but a dismal drip-drip on the flat sodden fields, endlessly day after day. So, too, drop by drop, our spirits oozed away. Faces and hearts fell as steadily as the rain itself.

We came to Oxford, with high hopes of drawing a big audience of scholars. But the Vice-Chancellor banned us, and we weren't allowed to set up our stage within the boundaries of the city. Undaunted, Desmond led us out to Abingdon, a market town in Berkshire only six miles away. He counted on a good crowd of the townspeople, together with scholars and citizens from Oxford who would make the journey if only to spite the Vice-Chancellor of the University.

But the luck was against us. The rain pelted down harder than ever, and the little wooded hills which rise from the Thames just there were blotted out by a yellow curtain of fog. There was almost no shelter for the audience, and barely a couple of dozen turned up. We called off the performance.

Half the company wanted to finish the tour there and then. It was no good, they argued. The season for open-air shows was over, the weather had broken, and it would be better to have the final share-out now, leaving each member to make his own way back to London as quickly as he liked. It was a waste of time to go on like this. They would only get back to London to find all the companies made up for the winter season and no parts left.

We all sat round a doleful little fire at the inn, and the smoke kept eddying back into our throats, choking us. I looked round at all their cross, gloomy faces and felt that my own fate was being decided.

Tomorrow I would be out of work.

I would be one of the thousands walking the roads of England . . . townsmen and countrymen alike, but mostly countrymen . . . I'd seen them every day, especially since the harvest had been gathered and there was less casual work to be found on the land. Some said it was the fault of the enclosures, driving men off the common lands. Some said sheep were to blame – one man can herd a great flock of them over an acreage which would give work to a dozen if it were under the plough. One man (and a learned one, an Oxford scholar) told Desmond it was all due to the Spaniards bringing too much silver from America, though how that put men out of work in Berkshire I couldn't understand.

Anyhow, the point was that I should soon be one of these workless, unwanted people, tramping along with winter at my heels.

Not only winter, but the Law.

The Law is harsh enough, God knows, to the ordinary man who finds no work. He is harried with heavy penalties, and if a crime is committed he is the first to be suspected. If suspected, he is as good as condemned, and if condemned, he is whipped and branded on the right ear. If he gets into trouble a second time the penalty is worse, and for a third offence it is death. There used to be hundreds of men hanged every year in the old Queen's day, and I doubt if many of them deserved it.

But I knew I should be in danger without that. The Poor Law says that an honest man who cannot find work may get relief from his own parish – but only from his own. Abingdon would not pay me a penny if I fell destitute there, nor would London. They would send me back to my own parish in Cumberland, to be helped by my neighbours – which would have been a fair enough arrangement if it hadn't meant delivering me straight into the arms of my enemy.

No, whatever happened, I thought to myself, I must never beg, never reveal myself as a pauper. Better to die of cold in a ditch . . .

The endless argument went on. At last I couldn't stand it any longer. I knew I had no voice in the matter – we boys held no shares in the company and couldn't vote – so I got up quietly and slipped from the room. The rain had stopped and the sun had peeped out, the first time for days, to bathe the town in red and gold.

I walked down the street with its cobbles flashing in the sunset, and stood on the long, narrow bridge. The Thames was brimming under the arches. There were swans. I looked across the vivid meadows, all silvered with flood-water, to a low hill that was golden with autumn woods. Suddenly I felt terribly home-sick – home-sick for the golden woods above Derwent-water, for the brimming silver floods lapping at the school-yard wall, and for my home at Lonsdale, with the low grey house bedded into the fellside, and the beck laughing at the foot of the slope, and Mother cooking something tasty on the hob. (They don't know how to eat in the south.)

If there had been only myself to think of, I would have started back that night and chanced the worst Sir Philip could do.

But there were others to think of – my father and

brother and all our neighbours who had met together that night to throw down the wall. So long as any evidence of mine could bring trouble on them, I must keep away.

It had seemed easy enough, the afternoon that I left. A strong, healthy boy, nearly a man, going off with money in his pocket – surely he could make his own way in the world for a year or two? How little we knew, in Lonsdale, of the big world that was hidden from us by our friendly fells!

'They've decided,' said a voice at my elbow. I turned. It was Kit Kirkstone.

'What?' I asked dully.

He came and leant on the bridge parapet beside me, and imitated me, spitting into the river. He could act, but he couldn't spit. It was a poor performance.

'We're winding up,' he said. 'They'll sell the wagons tomorrow, and share out. Desmond's taking two of the horses as his full share, and he and Mrs D. are off to London in the morning.'

'Oh,' I said.

'I'm going with them,' he went on. 'He says I can ride pillion behind him. He says he thinks he can get me a place along with them in Shakespeare's company. He says I've got such talent it would be a crime to leave me behind –'

'He says a lot,' I interrupted bitterly, all my old jealousy flaring up again. I had grown almost to like Kit the last week or two, feeling that we were companions in misfortune.

'You *are* jealous of me, aren't you?' he said thoughtfully.

'Jealous of you?' I jeered.

'It's not your fault you can't play heroines as well as I can,' he said, as cool as you please, as if there was no doubt of it – which to be quite honest there wasn't, but I wouldn't admit it at the time. 'I think you act wonderfully well,' he added graciously. 'Anyhow, I've told Mr Desmond I'll go with him on one condition – that he takes you too. I can ride behind Mrs Desmond if you'd sooner.'

What devil of pride made me flush with fury and tell him I didn't want his charity?

He shrugged his shoulders. 'It *is* a pity you're so conceited, Peter – I rather like you otherwise – but you're –'

I didn't let him finish. I'd never laid hands on him since that first morning we met, but now my self-control went. I landed out.

We swayed backwards and forwards on Abingdon Bridge in the twilight. I tried to box, to keep him at a distance, but it was mostly a helter-skelter, scrambling affair, regardless of rules. How foul he fought! My cheeks were streaming from his nails, and I think he bit me too – it was all too mixed up to be certain.

At last I managed to break away sufficiently to plant one other good blow – a breath-taking punch to the chest, which doubled him up like a jack-knife.

I looked down on him, moaning and twisting in the road, and wished I hadn't hit quite so hard. 'Perhaps that'll teach you,' I growled.

He didn't answer. I knelt down, rather scared now, and lifted his head from the ground.

Too late, I realized what I had done. I had solved the mystery of Kit Kirkstone.

8.

The Man from Stratford

I needn't have been quite so alarmed. Kit was only winded, and no more hurt than any boy would have been. Kneeling there on the damp cobbles, I stammered how sorry I was, how I'd never realized –

'You weren't meant to,' Kit muttered as the breath came back. 'Well, you know now. What are you going to do?'

'Do?'

'Yes, *do*. I'm at your mercy. You've only to tell Mr Desmond, and that's the finish of *my* career on the stage. It'll leave the field nice and clear for you, won't it?'

'You must think me pretty mean,' I protested.

I dabbed my bleeding cheek. All my temper had gone. I was feeling bad about it all. I'd hit a girl with all my force – but then it had never once occurred to me that Kit *was* a girl disguised, and not the boy she had always pretended to be. Afterwards, thinking back and remembering a dozen little things, I couldn't imagine why I'd never thought of it before, especially as the idea was always cropping up in the plays we acted. But I hadn't, and none of the others had ever suspected it either.

'It's not a question of meanness,' she said calmly. 'Who ever heard of a girl acting in the theatre? Perhaps *I'm* mean, coming along to take work away from boys. What do you think?'

I didn't answer for a few moments. She was right on one point – if the others found out she was a girl, it would be the finish of her acting. She would be pushed away behind the scenes with Mrs Desmond, with nothing more important to do than stitching and darning costumes. There would have been a fearful scandal if any of our audiences had realized that we had brought a young girl on to the public stage.

'It seems silly,' I said at last.

'Daft,' she agreed cheerfully.

'Why *shouldn't* women act women's parts?'

'Just what I say! It's a stupid, old-fashioned idea, not letting them. Men are scared that women would act them off the boards if they were given the chance!'

I couldn't allow that, and challenged it.

'Well, look at the old Queen!' she insisted triumphantly. 'There isn't an actor in the theatre can touch her.'

That rather shocked me. Up in Cumberland, Elizabeth seemed to me like a distant, unapproachable, and almost immortal goddess. It was only after a winter in London that I began to see her as the Londoners did – a flesh-and-blood, high-spirited old lady, with a sharp tongue and a gusty laugh. It's true she could have acted all the men out of the theatre. She could be dignified, tragic, pathetic, furious, witty, and (when she chose) almost comical. She could put on her mood like a mask to suit her company, be it an ambassador or a mayor, a countess or a chambermaid. But all this I was still to learn.

'I shan't tell anyone,' I said.

'You won't? Thanks, Peter. Ever so much.'

We had picked ourselves up now and were leaning on the parapet again. It was quite dark, but I didn't want to go back to the inn till I'd solved the mystery.

'What's your real name?' I asked.

'Kit. Only it's short for Katharine, not Christopher.'

'Won't you tell me your other name? I bet it isn't Kirkstone.'

She shook her head, but said nothing.

'You know, of course, mine's really Peter Brownrigg.'

'No. I thought it was Brown.'

'Honest?' I exclaimed. I remembered that letter . . . 'You mean to say you don't know all about me?'

'No, and I don't want to.' She added hurriedly: 'I don't mean to be rude, Peter. Only it's better for people to keep their own secrets.'

Still, there was one thing I had to know. 'You wrote to Sir Philip Morton,' I said accusingly. 'Why?'

'I know him. The letter was about . . . about my own affairs. Nothing to do with you. Why *should* it be?'

If she was going to keep her own secrets, so would I. I was sure, anyhow, that she was speaking the truth. It was fantastic that even Sir Philip should let a girl of thirteen travel the country for months with a crew of actors, if he knew where she was. And, if he did not know, she could hardly have betrayed me.

'I'll tell you something,' she said impulsively. 'It's only fair. But promise not to ask me more than I tell you.'

'I promise.'

'I've run away from home, for – for my own very good reasons. You remember that night you all stopped on the road between Penrith and Kendal, and lit a fire? That was the first time I saw you. I was hiding in the bracken. I'd run from home that evening, as soon as it was dark. When you moved on the next morning, I followed you. I saw my guardian stop you and search the wagons –'

'Your guardian?' I echoed.

'Yes. I have no father or mother. Or five sisters,' she

added, with a laugh. 'I had to invent them, to account for the way I knew how to curtsey and all that.'

I grinned. I knew I should never be jealous of Kit again. No wonder her acting had been so successful!

I could tell she wasn't going to say any more just then. It was late now, and one by one the lighted windows which overhung the river were disappearing. So we went back to the inn, had a word with Mr and Mrs Desmond (who looked curiously at our marked faces, but said nothing), and crawled into the wagon where the other boys were already asleep.

It was sad the next morning, saying good-bye to all the members of the company, even though we all promised each other that it was only for a few days and we should all be meeting in London before long. You couldn't get away from it – as a company we had ceased to exist. We weren't Mr Desmond's Famous Troop of London Players any longer, but a miscellaneous crowd of individuals, mostly rather shabby and down-at-heel.

Still, being young and very excited by the thought of seeing London even sooner than I expected, I didn't take it as seriously as some of the older men. I was in high spirits when I swung myself up behind Desmond and went clopping over the bridge along the Henley road.

It was a fine morning, for the rain had given over at last, and the whole world looked as though it had been washed and then polished by the sun. We rode through Dorchester, I remember, a place with a fine abbey church, and saw the high line of the Chilterns, red-gold with beech-woods, stretched between the green meadows and the egg-pale sky. We stopped at Henley for some ale, and I had a fancy that the Desmonds were looking at me in a queer way. Once, too, Kit gave me a most malignant scowl.

'*Idiot!*' she whispered hoarsely, seizing her chance when they were out of earshot.

'What's up?'

'Your fine manners!' she said, with infinite scorn. 'You've been speaking to me all the morning as though I were one of the Queen's waiting-women! You were going to help me on to the horse, only I dodged you. The Desmonds think you're cracked.'

'But –'

'You've got to forget I'm a girl. Treat me as you did before – no politeness, no favours. Be rude to me, bully me, do what you like, but for Heaven's sake don't give the game away. You ought to know by now that I can rough it as well as any of you.'

She could, too. I'd never heard her complain of anything. She could walk with the best of us, and there used to be plenty of walking, for, though people called us 'strolling players', we often covered fifteen or twenty miles between towns, with only an occasional ride on the wagon. Later, I was to hear something of her childhood, how she'd run wild for years, swimming and riding and climbing like a boy, so that it was easy for her to pretend to be one.

I mended my manners after Henley – or rather I changed them for the worse – and we slanged each other in the old way as we bumped along behind our friends. We couldn't see much of the country through which we passed, for both Mr and Mrs Desmond were broad in the back, and they blotted out all view of the road ahead.

We all felt happy that beautiful autumn afternoon. I was relieved because the shadow of Sir Philip Morton had been lifted from me, and, whatever troubles awaited us in London, I had confidence in the burly actor in front of me. He was in a cheerful mood himself, bellowing one song after another as the miles slowly unrolled beneath our horses' hooves. None of us thought that anything could possibly happen to us on that peaceful London road.

We came after a time to a river. There was a narrow bridge across it and a great congestion of traffic, for two long strings of pack-horses had met, travelling in opposite directions, and the merchants were cursing each other over the right-of-way. More travellers were piling up, snowball-like, at both bridgeheads – farm-carts and horsemen and a wonderful new carriage, belonging to some titled lady in a hurry to reach the Court. We stood for a few moments in the long line, till Desmond said impatiently:

'This is going to take all day; we might as well have gone by river-barge!'

A woman standing at her cottage door asked, Why didn't we try the old ford, down there? She pointed, and Desmond thanked her, and led us down a flagged path which ended in the river, just below the bridge.

'Is this the Thames?' called Mrs Desmond, rather more nervously than usual. Her husband laughed at her, for it was quite a narrow river (I forget even its name), a mere tributary. But it was running fast from the autumn rains, and I think, if I had seen it myself, instead of having my eyes fixed on the woollen cloak in front of me, I too might have had my doubts.

'It's not deep,' he called to her reassuringly. 'I've been this way before, now I remember. I'll go first.'

And in we went, with a good deal of snorting and splashing from the horse, and in a moment the muddy water was swirling round my ankles. I heard Desmond grunt surprisedly, and then, without ever quite knowing how it happened, I was in, head over heels.

I came up, spitting and spluttering, and found that the flooded river had already carried me out of my depth. The horse was floundering to safety in the shallows. Mrs Desmond was screaming on the bank. The bridge was lined with people hugely enjoying the accident.

But of Desmond, at first, I could see no sign. Then he suddenly bobbed to the surface a few feet away, and I saw that his eyes were closed. The current was sweeping him away like a log. I realized the horse must have kicked him when he first fell in.

I made straight for him, and clutched his hair as his face dipped under the water again. I wasn't frightened for myself but I doubted my strength to keep him up for long. The fools on the bridge still hadn't realized that anything was seriously the matter.

Then Kit arrived. She swam like an otter, and I saw at once that I needn't fear for her any more than for myself. I was thankful to see her, I can tell you: I'd never have managed it by myself. As it was, it took all our combined strength to steer him to the bank and get him out. We dropped beside him exhausted.

'He's all right,' I panted.

'Good!' All that worried Kit then was the changing

of her clothes, for people came running now from the cottages, offering help and dry things, and much as she wanted to strip off her soaked, clinging hose, she didn't want to do it in the middle of an admiring crowd. However, she'd got used to awkward moments like that, and now that I was her ally it was easier. I held everyone's attention with the story of how it happened, told already for the fourth time, while she sneaked away behind a haystack.

Desmond soon came round, but it proved that his leg was broken from the kick. We helped to make him comfortable in the nearest inn, and consoled Mrs Desmond as best we could, and then retired to a quiet corner to discuss the situation.

'He'll be here for weeks,' I said.

'What shall we do?' Kit asked. She said 'we', for I don't think it occurred to either of us that there was now very little to keep us together. We had lost the company, now we were losing the Desmonds, and for that very reason we both stuck closer than ever.

We decided to go on to London and try our luck alone.

Mrs Desmond agreed it was the best thing. She and her husband would have to stay where they were till his leg was mended; they would sell first one horse, then the other, if necessary, to pay for their board and lodging. Meantime, she would write a letter for us to take to Mr Burbage at the Globe Theatre, recommending our services to him. With this, and a couple of shillings which she insisted on sparing us from her thin purse, we took the road again the next morning.

It took us two days to reach London, though we got a ride or two on wagons. Kit knew London and said it was hard to sleep there without paying, so we gave up the idea of arriving on the second evening and slept under a hayrick instead, close to a village called Kensington. Then, waking in the crisp October dawn, we trudged up the Strand and saw, framed in the open gateway of Temple Bar, the great church of St Paul rising on its hill in the midst of the city.

Kit wasn't worried by the maze of narrow streets or the jostling thousands of people, and for the first time in our journey I let her take the lead.

'It's quite simple, really,' she said; 'we've only to keep straight on till we get to London Bridge, and then the theatre is just the other side.'

All the theatres were outside the City boundaries, so that the Lord Mayor could not forbid the performances. It'll give you some idea of how big London is if I say that there was not one theatre but several at this time, and in spite of the bear-gardens, cockpits, and other places of amusement there were always thousands of people to watch the plays.

Well, cutting a long story short, we arrived at the Globe, a fine new playhouse, only recently built for Burbage's company, who were known then as the Lord Chamberlain's Men. We asked for Mr Burbage, and were sent on to the Curtain Theatre, where the company had just moved for their winter season, since the Globe, though a splendid, up-to-date building, was open to the sky. The Curtain proved to be in Finsbury Fields, which meant a weary walk back across the bridge to the other side of London; but this time we were luckier, for a rehearsal was in progress.

Burbage came out to us after a few minutes, the letter crumpled in his hand. He was a tall, athletic fellow, with the devil of a temper, which he was showing now.

'What's this? What's this?' he stormed, almost as if we had kicked Desmond ourselves and broken his leg. 'Desmond injured? Won't be in London for a month? I wanted that man. I needed him. Tell him he's *got* to get better. I want him on this stage if he has to walk with two sticks! Tell him that!'

Kit spoke before I could find my tongue. 'But we're not going back,' she pointed out sweetly.

'What?' He glanced at the letter and snorted. 'Oh no, I see. Mrs Desmond wondered if I could give you parts

. . . You saved Desmond's life . . . What the devil was the use of that, if you let the fat fool break his leg?' He crumpled up the letter finally, and ground it under his heel. With it he ground my heart and my hopes.

'What does she take my theatre for – a school?' he demanded. 'Boys, boys, boys! Everyone sends me boys. Do they imagine I eat boys for breakfast? They can't possibly think I use 'em any other way. Boys, boys – long boys and short boys, cheeky boys and weepy boys, they're driving me mad as it is. And each fresh one acts worse than the one before.' He made a gesture of finality, and began to shoo us out of the building.

I stood my ground. 'We're different,' I began.

'They're *all* different,' he retorted, 'different as rotten apples – the rotten patch varies in each –'

'You should try him, anyhow – he's good,' I said, all in a rush. 'You should have heard the crowd at Lancaster and Preston and Manchester –'

He laughed contemptuously. 'I've no doubt he squeaked and lisped very prettily. But what does for the little places like Manchester won't go down in London.'

'You mean you won't try us?' said Kit.

'Sorry, I haven't time, and it really wouldn't be any use. We're not wanting boys of your type. Good day.'

And that was that. 'Never mind,' said Kit, taking my arm as we walked off, 'there *are* other theatres.'

There were, and we tried them one by one. We went back to Southwark to the Rose. We visited the Swan in Paris Garden, and the Blackfriars, which we heard was often used by companies made up entirely of boys. Surely we should find work *there*. But nothing came of it, and it was the same dismal tale when we tried the St Paul's Playhouse, close by the great church. We hadn't been to St Paul's School, and they didn't want us in the boys' company there. They pretended they couldn't understand our Cumberland speech.

So there we were. Nobody wanted us, and we'd only a few shillings between us and starvation. If we couldn't find work of the kind we *could* do, what chance had we of branching out in a fresh occupation?

We sat down, miserable and aching in every bone, on a bench in front of an alehouse in Fleet Street. Soon we were thinking of lodging for the night and something to eat. We'd had no meal since early morning, we'd been so hot on the trail of work.

Kit quoted bitterly:

> *'Now is the winter of our discontent*
> *Made glorious summer –'*

'I *don't* think,' I grunted.

A youngish man, standing in the alehouse doorway, gave us a sharp glance and stepped towards us. 'How are you getting on?' he asked pleasantly.

We started. It was the first kind remark made to us since we entered the City.

'I saw you this morning, talking to Burbage at the theatre,' he explained.

'Oh, do you act?' said Kit eagerly.

'I try,' said the man, with a twinkle in his eye. 'But,' he added modestly, 'I never get any of the big parts.'

'We'd be glad of any part,' I put in. 'We've tried everywhere. They won't even listen to us.'

'I know.' He looked grave and sympathetic now. 'It's hard when you first come up here from the country. I've had some myself.' Then he smiled again, and pulled a roll of script from his doublet. 'It shan't be said you haven't had a hearing at all. Can you read my writing?'

It was pretty bad – the writing, I mean, but we managed. I felt rather listless about it myself. This man had admitted that he was only a minor actor, and I couldn't see how much it would help us even if he liked our reading. But Kit read as she always did when she got a script in her hands – as if her heart and soul were in it:

'Come, night; come, Romeo; come, thou day in night;
For thou wilt lie upon the wings of night
Whiter than new snow on a raven's back . . .'

'Good,' said the young man hoarsely when she finished. 'Do you know, you're the first boy who hasn't murdered that speech – simply *murdered* it?'

'What a shame! It's *beautiful.*'

'Do you think so? Really?' The man looked pleased. 'Look here, come inside and we'll discuss matters over a bite of supper. Perhaps I can help you, after all. What are your names? Where do you come from? I'm from Stratford myself – my name's Shakespeare.'

9.

Re-enter Danger!

I think Will Shakespeare was the most *understanding* person I ever knew.

He was in his thirties then, with all his glory still ahead of him; but to us, so much younger, he seemed to have had a lifetime of experience. Like me, he had come up to London to make his fortune – though it is a lie, I am sure, that he had run from Stratford, as I from Cumberland, in fear of the law. But he was a countryman, and knew what it was to shear sheep and cart hay. He would catch my eye sometimes when I was in a home-sick mood, and give me a glance as much as to say: I know what it is.

He feasted us handsomely that night, for, as he told us, he had just finished a new play and the company had paid him six pounds for it. I can see his face now, bending across the loaded table, the candlelight dancing in his deep eyes and on his great forehead, from which the dark hair was already receding.

He listened to all our tales of Desmond's company, and laughed when he heard of our poor reception at Stratford-upon-Avon. He laughed again, more ruefully, when he heard that our most popular play was his own *Two Gentlemen of Verona*.

'They're all doing my plays now,' he said, 'and I never get a penny except from my own company. They'd steal even my new plays if they could lay hands on them. Pirates, I call them – pirates of the playhouse.'

We drank in all he told us, for every scrap of knowledge about the London theatres was welcome to such a stage-struck pair as we. We felt that everything was going to be all right now. Shakespeare filled our stomachs with supper and our hearts with hope. At last, when we were nodding in our seats, he called the landlord, arranged for us to sleep free of charge that night, and told us to ask for him at the Curtain Theatre tomorrow.

It was very different, that second visit.

Burbage was as sunny as June, and greeted us as if we had never met before. 'Which is your wonderful Juliet?' he asked.

'This one,' said Shakespeare, pushing Kit forward and handing him the play. 'Listen.' Kit read:

> *'Farewell! God knows when we shall meet again.*
> *I have a faint cold fear thrills through my veins,*
> *That almost freezes up the heat of life . . .'*

When he had finished, Burbage slapped his thigh and swore delightedly. 'Yes! And he'll look the part, too, by thunder!' Then he turned doubtfully to me, standing there with my scratched face. 'What about this one? *He's* no Italian beauty.'

'He's a born mimic,' said Shakespeare. 'You should have heard him last night, spinning yarns of the Desmonds' summer tour, taking off all the people they met. Here, Peter, read the part of Juliet's Nurse, and make her the funniest, gossipiest old creature you've ever known.'

I did my best, though it's hard trying to be funny in front of two or three people. Still, I seemed to satisfy them, for Burbage agreed to take me into the company. I couldn't play the Nurse yet, for they had a good boy in the part already, but I could walk on in small parts like Lady Montague and understudy the bigger ones in case another boy fell ill.

We both became Shakespeare's apprentices. The company paid him for our work at the rate of four shillings a week each, and he handed the whole of it over to us. He, and most of the other regular grown-up actors, held shares in the company and divided the profits accordingly. When we were older we might become sharers too, by paying money into the pool, or we might be taken on as 'hirelings', earning a weekly wage of anything from five to eight shillings.

Now, with eight shillings a week between us, we could just live. With Shakespeare's help, we found a little garret not far from the theatre, and he told us the cheapest places to buy our food. London was a cold, hungry place that winter, with fogs rising from the river to join the smoke-pall thickened by a thousand chimneys. How I longed, sometimes, for a bright, sweet-smelling fire of peat from Skiddaw and a few slices of my mother's mutton hams!

I had a letter from her, early in December, brought by a pedlar to the Flower de Luce Tavern, where I collected it a few days later. It had been written on 22 November.

'You will do well to keep away, at any rate until the spring' [she wrote], 'for things are more bitter than ever between us and Sir Philip. He began to rebuild his wall in October. John Keld – you know his temper! – went to stop him, and the end of the matter was a fight, with one of Sir Philip's servants half-drowned in the river. John Keld has left home for the present, and we think he is in Scotland. There seems no end to Sir Philip's ambition; he has enclosed some meadows on the Penrith side of the estate, and the meek fools never raised a finger to stop him. He is making money hand over fist, and people say he means to make himself one of the biggest men in Cumberland. But not all his little plans have come off as he liked, and there are some good chuckling tales going round the farms, which you shall hear when you come home . . .'

There was a lot then about the family and the farm, with news of all the neighbours and our animals, especially the old pony. Besides the letter, there was a big parcel with a piece of that very mutton ham for which I'd been longing, a pot of sweet butter, and other Cumberland dainties which Kit enjoyed as much as I did. 'Nice, having a mother,' she said.

Those were busy days.

We had so many parts to learn, especially Kit. The Lord Chamberlain's Men had a host of plays in their repertory – comedies, histories, and tragedies, not only by Shakespeare, but by Marlowe, the new playwright Ben Jonson, and half a dozen others. Almost every day we played a different piece, sometimes a new one, sometimes one that hadn't been acted for months or even years. One day we might have quite big parts, and the next have not a line to say. Kit might just sweep across the stage in silence, looking divinely beautiful as the Spirit of Helen of Troy in *Doctor Faustus*, and I might appear as one of the Seven Deadly Sins (Gluttony, usually, with a great padded belly and a mask!), or I might have nothing to do but move furniture on the stage and hold up a board saying: 'A Street in London' or 'A Battlefield'.

It wasn't for weeks that Kit was able to make her first appearance as Juliet. By that time the Desmonds had arrived, fatter and jollier than ever, and been received into the company with open arms. But I could see that, popular as he was, Desmond was only second-rate beside Burbage and the other leading men.

Everyone was certain that Kit, as Juliet, would be the sensation of the town. Her other performances had been clapped to the echo – people were talking of the wonderful new boy-actor from the North – but she hadn't really had a chance to spread her wings yet. *Romeo and Juliet* was to provide that chance. It was Shakespeare's best play; Burbage was to be Romeo, and we all felt sure that, once news of the performance reached the Queen, we should get a command to take the play to Court.

The great day dawned.

'Nervous?' I asked, with a laugh, because I knew she wasn't – she never was.

She shook her head.'I wish you were Nurse, though,' she said;'you're twice as funny in the part as Mortimer – he's like cold pudding. I'd act better with you, Pete.'

'Thanks! Well, maybe Mortimer will slip on some orange-peel; I know his part if he does, and yours too for that matter.'

It was true. Standing there day after day at rehearsals, and hearing Kit repeating her lines in our garret, I had come to know every word of it. But there, anyone can learn lines. Neither I nor any other boy in the theatre could say them, look them, and live them, as Kit could.

We went along to the Curtain together. People were streaming in by the hundred. Hot chestnuts were on sale at the door, mulled ale, and other good things to keep the cold out. The pit was full. Gentlemen were paying as much as a shilling to hire stools on the stage, so that they could study the new 'Juliet' at close range. How I hated the practice! Sometimes they so packed the sides of the stage that there was barely room to act, and all the time one was conscious of their whisperings and nudgings and the tobacco smoke they puffed into one's face. I was sorry that Kit should have to act under such difficult conditions.

I had put on my heavy costume – I was playing Lady Montague, and I was supposed to be the mother of great Burbage! – when I found Kit at my elbow, her eyes like harvest moons. She too had dressed (the company had bought magnificent new costumes for the occasion), but she was tearing at the fastening with panic-stricken fingers.

'What's the matter?' I demanded.

'I can't go on,' she stammered, letting her great golden farthingale flop to the ground, and kicking her feet out of it.

'Can't go *on*?'

I couldn't believe my ears. After all her other successes, surely she hadn't been gripped by stage fright? I don't think she knew the meaning of the word.

'Let's get out of here,' she said wildly, and ran from the room in her shirt and hose, still wearing Juliet's golden slippers. I rushed after her, but, hampered as I was in my billowing farthingale and the high heels to which I could never get quite accustomed, I hadn't the remotest chance of catching her.

Just then Burbage came along. 'Where's Kit? Why is his costume kicking about on the ground?'

I told him.

He swore terribly. I quaked in my little high-heeled shoes.

'Search the building!' he bellowed at last, in a voice which shook the roof, and then, as men ran to obey, he cursed them for making so much noise. Didn't they realize the audience were just in front there, and would hear every sound?

I gathered up the lovely golden farthingale. I knew they wouldn't find Kit. She didn't mean to be found. But Dick Prior, her understudy, would be wanting the costume quickly.

Burbage came storming back. 'Get into that thing,' he ordered.

'But I – I – that is, Dick Prior –'

'Get into it! Don't argue! Prior cleared off as soon as Kirkstone arrived. How was he to know he'd be wanted? Kirkstone looked fit as a fiddle half an hour ago. You know the lines, don't you?'

'Yes, sir –'

'Then say them, for pity's sake, say them.' He clapped his hand to his brow, tragically. 'That's all you need do. The show's ruined. We'll be lucky if they don't burn the theatre to the ground.'

Willing hands helped me into Juliet's costume, fitted my wig, painted my lips and cheeks, and tried to perform the impossible task of making me look beautiful. We could hear, through the curtains that the play had begun, and that so far it was going excellently.

Shakespeare's hand was on my shoulder. His pale face masked his disappointment. 'Don't let them worry you,' he murmured. 'Remember, you *can* act. And the moon's fine to look at – when the sun isn't there.'

'I'll do my best,' I said.

The moment had come for my first entrance. I heard my cue, the Nurse shouting: 'Where's this girl? What, Juliet!'

I held up my skirts and slipped through the gap in the curtains. I heard my own voice, thin and clear: 'How now! Who calls?' and then I heard the murmur of surprise and disappointment run round the theatre. It stung my pride. All right, I'd show them I too could act.

I lifted my head proudly to face the whispering gentlemen on their stools . . .

And looked straight into the eyes of Sir Philip Morton!

10.

Sir Philip is the Man

He sat there in his crimson velvet doublet, one black leg crossed over the other, his thin lips parted above his golden beard as he sucked the stem of his tobacco-pipe. There was surprise in his cold blue eyes, but it was not the surprise of recognition – only the surprise of hundreds of others that afternoon, that Juliet was not to be played by the good-looking boy who had become the talk of the town.

He did not know me – yet.

Would his memory be stirred before the long play was over? Would some trick of my walk or my voice – my voice especially, which had never lost its Cumberland ring – start a train of recollection in his mind which would mean disaster? I can only play on, I thought to myself, and hope for the best; with this wig and make-up and these flouncing clothes I must look utterly different from the boy he saw in the dawn-light under Blencathra and chased through the Penrith inn.

I'd watched Kit play the part so often at rehearsals, and she used to act as though she were inspired – as though she *were* Juliet, living it all, instead of Kit Kirkstone pretending. I couldn't act like that to save my life, but, as Shakespeare said, I *was* a pretty good mimic. I remembered the way Kit used to speak each line, the words she stressed, the rise and fall of her voice. I knew her moves, too, and the way she looked when she spoke certain lines, and all her by-play with hands and handkerchiefs and the dagger at the end.

My Juliet was like a looking-glass reflection of hers.

That is a perfect comparison. There wasn't the depth in my acting, but at least it looked all right.

At first I was acting for only one member of the audience – Sir Philip. I knew that my safety depended on my complete concealment of Peter Brownrigg. Sir Philip must see me only as Juliet.

But as the afternoon wore on, and the spectators lost their original disappointment and grew more friendly, I began to forget my danger and play, as a good actor should, for the whole audience. At my second exit there was a real round of applause, which warmed me as a glass of wine would have done. Burbage encouraged me in a gruff whisper, Shakespeare tweaked my ear affectionately. The situation was saved – so far as the play was concerned. Sir Philip was another matter.

His eyes were on me the whole time I was on the stage. Sometimes my acting brought me within a pace or two of his outstretched foot. Once his tobacco set me coughing in the middle of a long speech. He muttered an apology, and immediately tapped out his pipe against his heel.

Yes, it was lucky for me that Sir Philip, with all his faults, was a true lover of the theatre. He enjoyed our show that afternoon. Had he been bored, his mind might have started idly wandering, and goodness knows to what perilous conclusions it might have come!

As it was, when I finally drove my blunt stage-dagger into the folds of my dress, and subsided carefully and gracefully on Burbage's chest, I felt pretty certain that all was well.

I got a shock a minute or two later. No sooner had my 'corpse' been ceremoniously carried off the stage by the Prince's attendants (and rather less ceremoniously set down on its feet in the wings!) than a hefty fellow tapped me on the shoulder.

'Juliet?' he enquired.

'Yes.'

'I'm groom to Sir Philip Morton.'

'Yes?' I braced myself for flight, but I knew it would be difficult in my stage-clothes.

'Sir Philip liked your acting,' said the groom.

'He – he doesn't want to see me, does he? I couldn't possibly –'

'See you?' The man snorted. 'What would he want to see a boy like you for? No; he just told me to give you this.'

And he walked off, with his bow-legged groom's walk, leaving me with a box of sweets in my hand. I looked after him, speechless, and, when he had gone, everyone wondered why I burst out laughing and leant back against the wall, unable to stop.

Five minutes later, when I had just stepped out of my costume and was standing in my own short pants and shirt, Burbage appeared.

'Good lad,' he said briefly. 'You just saved us.'

I should have been immensely pleased, but I saw a look in his eye.

'Where's that rascal?' he demanded.

'Who d'you mean?' I said stupidly, knowing only too well.

'I'm going to thrash him within an inch of his life,' he said with a terrible gusto, and I knew he meant it.

I put my feet into my hose, pulled them up, and began

fastening the points at my waist line. I was wondering what had happened to Kit. Had she gone home? That was the best place for her till Burbage's wrath had abated. He wasn't safe company at present.

'I think she – he wasn't feeling well,' I started, but Burbage cut me short.

'Don't make excuses for the little beast!' he raged. 'There *is* no excuse for throwing up a part without notice. If the cursed boy didn't act like a – like an angel, I'd throw him out neck and crop, and never let him set foot in the theatre again. As it is, I'm going to give him the thrashing of his misspent life.'

Kit chose that very moment to swagger in, looking as pleased as if she'd just laid an egg. All her fear had gone. She was on top of the world.

'Congratulations, Pete! You –'

Then she saw Burbage turning grimly to face her, and her jaw dropped.

'You'd better run, Kit!' I shouted. But Burbage stepped between her and the door.

'*Well?*' he said, and that one syllable held as much terror as a sentence of execution.

'I'm so sorry, sir,' said Kit, 'but you see –'

'You are *going* to be sorry,' he corrected her. 'Very sorry. Sorrier than you have ever been about anything in your life.'

'But – but,' she stammered, 'Peter was so good –'

'He might not have been,' said Burbage. 'You didn't know.' He moved slowly towards her, his hands outstretched.

'You mustn't,' I shouted, clutching his arm. 'You mustn't really, Mr Burbage. Listen. Kit isn't –'

'Shut up, Peter!' said Kit fiercely. She was determined to take what was coming to her. Perhaps she thought it was going to be a mere spanking; I think she had never seen a boy thrashed by an angry man till the blood flows.

'Get out of the way,' said Burbage quietly, and with one jerk of his arm he sent me tumbling into a corner. He was towering above her now. 'You disobedient, worthless, disloyal, irresponsible, ungrateful, unprofessional –'

'What's this?' Shakespeare's voice came smoothly from the doorway. 'Is this a new punishment, Dick? Sentenced to receive a hundred and one adjectives! Better than strokes, anyhow.'

'He's going to get the strokes as well.'

Shakespeare crossed the room and took his friend gently by the arm. 'No, Dick.'

'Leave this to me, Will. You're too kind-hearted. The young actor scoundrel must have his lesson. The first rule of an actor is never to let down his company.'

Shakespeare didn't move from his side. 'If anyone is to teach him the rules of acting, let it be I.'

'You? My dear Will, you may write like the Muse herself, but when it comes to *acting* –'

'I bow to you every time,' Shakespeare admitted, with a smile. 'None the less, these two boys are my apprentices. No one else in the company lays a finger on them.'

'All right.' Burbage stepped back with a shrug of his shoulders. 'So be it. But it's your job to keep your apprentices in order. If we have any more of this nonsense, out of the company they go.'

'Leave them to me. There will be no more nonsense.'

Burbage stalked out. Kit looked at Shakespeare meekly.

'Are *you* going to thrash me?'

He laughed. 'You know perfectly well I'm not – my dear.'

We both gasped, Kit and I. He closed the door and motioned to us to sit down.

'I guessed some days ago,' he said. 'No boy could have played Juliet as you did. Though,' he added, with a friendly glance at me, 'Peter *echoed* you very cleverly. Now, won't you tell me all about it?'

And, to my amazement, Kit (who had kept so many secrets from me all this time) poured out her whole story. As I said before, Shakespeare was an understanding man. You felt you could tell him things.

'I was a bit like Juliet,' she said. 'I s'pose that's why the part came easy to me. My guardian wanted me to marry a man I didn't like –'

'You're young,' said Shakespeare, raising his eyebrows.

'Thirteen. Nearly as old as Juliet. Anyhow, the wedding wasn't to be for a year or two, but the formal engagement was all planned ready.'

'And Romeo?' The author's eyes twinkled.

Kit laughed scornfully. 'There wasn't any Romeo. I don't want to marry *anybody*. So all I did was to run away from my guardian's house one evening as soon as it was dark, and then I joined Desmond's company as a boy, and you know all the rest. I mean to stop away from home till I'm old enough to please myself, and not be bullied by any of them.'

'I pity the man who marries you against your will,' chuckled Shakespeare.

'Why should he *want* to?' I asked. It sounded daft to me.

'It may surprise you to know,' said Kit, turning to me with great dignity, 'but I'm extraordinarily well connected. And when I come of age I inherit a magnificent estate.'

'So *there*!' cried Shakespeare, with a triumphant grin. 'Now we know why the man wanted such a quaint little imp for his wife.'

'Pig!' she said.

'You still haven't explained, Miss Katharine Russell, why you were seized with panic just before the play began and risked ruining our whole performance.'

'I'm terribly sorry,' she answered, and for the first time she looked genuinely ashamed of herself. 'I was so frightened I forgot everything else.'

'But why?'

'The man who wants to marry me was in the audience. I knew he'd recognize me at once if he saw me dressed as a girl.'

'What's his name?' asked Shakespeare.

'I know!' I cried, seeing daylight suddenly. 'Sir Philip Morton!'

11.

The House of the Yellow Gentleman

It was good to have finished with secrets, at any rate between Kit and me and our friend. When Kit heard the full story of my own dealings with Sir Philip, she was full of apologies for sending me into the danger she had avoided herself. But, as I pointed out, the cases were different. I, as Juliet looked utterly unlike myself. Kit, in the same costume, looked far more like Katharine Russell than ever she did in her everyday disguise as a boy.

'The man's a brute,' she said viciously. 'He doesn't care twopence about me, really – treats me as a child. All he wants to do is to lay hands on my estate. That's why he tried to fix up a formal public engagement before I was old enough to realize how serious it all was. He thought I wouldn't dare break it off, and soon as I was fifteen or so he'd marry me and take everything.'

'What was your guardian thinking of?' asked Shakespeare.

She shrugged her shoulders. 'I don't know. Mr Norman used to be so nice; he was Dad's best friend. But since he got in with Sir Philip . . .' She paused, and actually shivered. 'Sir Philip's queer. He seems to have a power over people. He's the only man I've ever met who really scares me.'

Shakespeare thought for a moment, stroking his tiny pointed beard. 'I'll speak to the doorman,' he said at length. 'If Sir Philip comes to the theatre again, you'll get word at once and you won't go on. It's a confounded nuisance, but it's better than losing you entirely.'

'What about Mr Burbage?'

'I'll speak to him, too. No, I won't tell him about you, my dear; that's a secret best locked in our bosoms. But I'll think of something.' He chuckled. 'They all make fun of me, you know, because I never invent my own stories for my plays. But I'll cook up some tale, never you fear.'

Luckily, our anxiety was soon removed, for two days later we heard that Sir Philip had left his lodgings for Cumberland, and it was not likely that he would make the long journey again for many a day. I think that, much as he liked London life, he wasn't too popular with the old Queen and did not move in Court circles. He wasn't a man who could bear to play second fiddle to anyone, so for the most part he preferred to busy himself in Cumberland, where he certainly had plenty to do, what with stealing common lands, scheming to marry heiresses, and practising even more ambitious villainies which at that time we didn't suspect.

It was fine to know that he was safely started on the long northward road. We didn't realize how soon his shadow was to fall across our path again . . .

Kit played Juliet at last. The town went mad over her – as we'd known they would. Even Burbage, as Romeo, was quite eclipsed, but he was too great a player to be jealous. That night he and Shakespeare took us out to supper at a tavern, and we ate till it was a wonder our skins didn't split like sausages. Burbage got sad after a few glasses of wine and looked mournfully at Kit.

'It was great acting,' he admitted, 'but what future has the boy got?'

'What future?' Shakespeare echoed.

The manager sighed. 'All very nice – pretty as a girl – the best boy we've ever had for the part. But you know how they all go.' He turned to Kit and addressed her solemnly. 'In another year or two, young man, you'll be sprouting black hairs on your lip and chin, and your voice will crack. Of course, you *may* get over it, and blossom forth in male parts; but somehow they never do, they never do . . . I can see you as Juliet, but never as Romeo.'

Shakespeare was chuckling. 'Don't meet your troubles half-way, Dick. I'll bet you a pound that Kit has no beard ten years from now.'

'No, thanks.' Burbage poured himself more wine. 'The theatrical business is the only gamble I touch – and it's quite enough, believe me.'

'But who'd give it up?' said Desmond challengingly.

'I would.' That was Shakespeare. We all looked at him.

'You?' cried Burbage. 'But, man, you're going to be great; you're writing as well as Marlowe now. You may even write better some day. You wouldn't give it all up?'

'I think so . . . when I'm ready.' Shakespeare looked into the crackling fire, and as he went on quietly talking I knew he was looking straight through the flames and the black chimney into Warwickshire. 'That house I bought last year at Stratford –'

'New Place?'

'Yes. That's the home for me, not those poky rooms in Bishopsgate. I want a garden. I want a river; the Thames isn't a river here; it's a street and a sewer and a cemetery!' He turned suddenly to me. 'What do you say, Peter? Where do you mean to end your days? London – or Cumberland?'

I smiled at him, and we seemed like two countrymen meeting in a city crowd. I thought of Blencathra under a blue satin sky, and Skiddaw Forest when the heather is new, and Derwentwater mirroring all the fells, and young larches standing out against a hillside sugared with snow . . . and a thousand such things. And I said huskily: 'Cumberland, please God!'

'Me, too,' said Kit. I felt very glad that she agreed with me.

Not that London wasn't a grand place just then, with Christmas coming and the Lord Chamberlain's Men commanded to act before the Queen at Court on Twelfth Night. That was the climax of nearly a fortnight's hard work and festivities: when we weren't acting to crammed, good-natured audiences, we were enjoying ourselves at Shakespeare's place in Bishopsgate, or the Desmonds' rooms at the Flower de Luce, or skating on the ponds out Kensington way. But I shall never forget Twelfth Night at Whitehall Palace, with our stage set in the great hall. It was all hung with holly and ivy and bays and rosemary and mistletoe, and a thousand candles winking on the ladies' jewels, and the Queen sitting just in front of us, her silken skirts curving out around her like a cascade of silver, her great ruff framing her face like a halo . . . We did Shakespeare's *Merry Wives of Windsor*, which he had written to please her, because she wanted to see the fat man, Falstaff, in love. Kit was Anne Page and I was Mistress Quickly. Several times I made the Queen herself laugh right out loud. We got ten pounds for the whole show, which was good, but nothing extraordinary. The Queen was very economical, and felt that we really ought to be satisfied with the advertisement we got through being her favourite actors. It didn't make any difference to us apprentices, anyhow; what pleased us was the marvellous food they gave us, dishes left over from the banquet – roast peacock and swan, buttered oranges, tansy, and 'snow', which was mostly cream, sugar, and white of egg, and slipped down very pleasantly when we were stuffed with the heavier things. It's true I was rather ill during the night afterwards, and Kit called me a fat Christmas hog, but it was worth it.

Winter passed, and spring followed. Soon we should move to our summer quarters, the new Globe Theatre. Shakespeare was writing a play about King Henry the Fifth, which was likely to be popular because war was in the news that year, owing to Lord Essex's campaign in Ireland. Kit was to be the French Princess Katharine, for she had to talk French, which she did easily, because she'd had a good tutor at home. I was Mistress Quickly again, for she came into the new play, too, and I'd made rather a speciality of her character. We hoped that with any luck we'd get a command to play before the Queen.

I remember we got our copies of the script just after May Day. And a strange thing happened, which set a number of other strange things in motion.

Perhaps I ought to explain that by this time we were quite well-known London characters – anyhow, in the two theatre districts of Finsbury and Southwark, and, of course, among the courtiers and fashionable people who came regularly to see our company. That's why I thought nothing amiss when the yellow gentleman started to speak to me outside St Paul's. It was quite usual for perfect strangers to greet us, and say something complimentary.

I didn't know his name, but I called him the yellow gentleman because of his yellow doublet, all slashed very fashionably, in some material that must have cost a fortune. He looked a very fine person, and I was fool enough to feel quite flattered to be seen talking to him.

'Mistress Quickly, I think?' he said, with a smile. 'And Juliet's Nurse, and Lucetta, and –' He rattled off half a dozen parts I regularly played. 'And what are you at work on now?'

I told him about *Henry the Fifth* – there was no secret about it – and the probable date of the first performance. He looked disappointed.

'What a pity! I shall miss it. I shall be in Italy by then. Is this the script?'

I passed it to him. He scanned the opening lines.

> *'O, for a muse of fire, that would ascend*
> *The brightest heaven of invention! . . .'*

he read softly under his breath. 'Magnificent stuff!' he exclaimed. 'How like my luck to miss it!' He read on silently, fairly eating the play. At last he lifted his eyes with a sigh. 'I suppose you couldn't spare this copy, just for this evening? If I can't see it, I *should* like to read it.'

It was difficult to refuse. Anyhow, he gave me a shilling. If shillings are as scarce in your life as they are in mine, you'd have done the same.

He'd only just left me when Kit came along; we'd arranged to meet in St Paul's Churchyard, and of course she was late. That was the one trick of hers she could never get rid of.

'Idiot! Country bumpkin!' she said pleasantly when she heard. 'What was his name? Where does he live or lodge?'

'I – I didn't ask.'

'Oh, *Peter*! You do need me to look after you!'

'It's quite all right,' I protested. 'He's going to meet

me here, in the very same spot, tomorrow morning at nine.'

'He never will,' she said decidedly.

Nor did he. Kit came with me to keep the appointment, and we waited till the clock struck ten, but the yellow gentleman did not appear.

'He's a pirate,' said Kit, 'a playhouse pirate. He'll sell that play to someone else, and they'll rush it into production and do it before we do.'

I began to have a terrible conviction that she was right. I wondered how on earth I should confess to Shakespeare that I had sold his new play for a shilling.

'Cheer up,' said Kit. 'I may be wrong. He may have overslept or something. Anyhow, he knows who *you* are, and if he's honest he can return the script to you at the theatre.'

Of course he didn't. And we both knew he wouldn't. There seemed nothing left to do but go to Shakespeare and confess. If *he* thought the yellow gentleman was a pirate, he could hurry on our own production and bring it out before the others. That would be a great pity though, because it was now practically fixed that the first performance should be given to the Queen, and that date couldn't be altered because the Court was on one of its periodical 'progresses', or tours, round the country.

We were walking down Fleet Street, Kit and I, thrashing out the matter for the sixteenth time, and I had just said I'd go straight to Bishopsgate and tell him, when – wonder of wonders! – I saw the yellow gentleman.

'There he is!' I cried, and grabbed her arm.

'Where? Who? Oh, I see.'

He was riding the other way, out of the city. I shouted, but the rumble of carts and the cries of the shopmen were too loud. He rode on without turning his head.

'After him,' I gasped, and we began to trot, threading our way through the passers-by and the bales of merchandise on the pavement. Mounted though he was, he could be overtaken if we hurried. Until he was through Temple Bar, and well along the Strand, he couldn't canter. Of course, if he reached the open country, we'd never catch him.

There was a jam of traffic at Temple Bar. He had to rein in his horse and wait behind a farm-cart until a squadron of soldiers had ridden through the narrow gate. I seized my chance, slipped between a carriage and a man with a donkey, and reached his side.

'Excuse me, sir –'

He looked down from his saddle. For a moment his eyes flashed recognition instinctively. Then he remembered – and pretended not to remember.

'What do you want, my lad?'

'I lent you a copy of a play –'

'You *what*? What's the matter? Are you crazy? You're mistaking me for someone else.'

'Oh no, I'm not,' I said firmly, and grasped his bridle. At least now I knew I was dealing with a thief, not a forgetful gentleman, and I could behave straightforwardly.

He cut me across the shoulders with his whip, but I still held his bridle, and a crowd began to gather. One of the gate-keepers bustled forward, swearing because the traffic block was being worsened. I stuck to my story. It was gospel truth, and I couldn't understand why everyone else couldn't see it was gospel truth.

Looking back now I can see it with their eyes. A gentleman on a horse – and an actor boy, a vagabond, shouting absurd accusations about stolen plays. (How could you steal a play – or who would want to? And the boy didn't even know the name of the gentleman he was accusing!)

Yes, I can understand better now why they dragged me away, sent me flying into the gutter, and yelled after me that I was lucky not to be handed over to the Law for a thrashing.

When I picked myself up, red with shame and fury, the yellow gentleman had gone. So, to my surprise, had Kit. She hadn't said a word to back up my story, she hadn't even stayed to console me. I felt deserted and resentful.

I did her an injustice. She came walking through the gate, glared at the keeper, stuck out her tongue at the passers-by who had lingered and were still grinning, and then led me away without a word. From the way she squeezed my arm I knew that there was still hope.

'I've found out where he lives,' she said as soon as we'd gone a safe distance.

'I wondered where on earth you'd got to.'

'Well, I knew I couldn't help you,' she said sensibly. 'If bull-at-a-gate methods were going to do the trick, I knew you'd manage without me. But I had a fancy things would turn out as they did, so I kept in the background. He didn't know I was with you. He looked back once, to make sure you weren't following him, but he didn't give me a glance. Then he rode through a gate, and I could see from the way the servant took his horse that he's staying there, even if it isn't his own home.'

'Where was it? Along the Strand?'

'Just off. Right down on the river-bank. One of those houses that rise straight from the water, I should think. Not a very big one – or it looks small, because it's wedged in between two huge places.'

'Well, thanks; it was pretty smart of you,' I said doubt-fully, 'but I don't quite see what the next move is.'

Kit admitted that she didn't either. 'Still,' she argued, 'it's something to know where the man's to be found, and to know that the play is somewhere inside that house.'

'And I'm going to get it back,' I vowed, though for the life of me I couldn't see how. There was no sense in going to knock on the front door and asking for it. If it had been money or jewels, I suppose we could, with Shakespeare's help, have got a magistrate's warrant to search the house. But would any Justice of the Peace help us to look for a lost play? Yet, the more I thought the matter over the more important it seemed that we should regain the script. The yellow gentleman had behaved so suspiciously.

I began to wonder if I could get into that house, without anyone's warrant or permission, and recover what was (after all) only my own property.

We walked back, looking as if butter wouldn't melt in our mouths, and I peeped at the house Kit indicated. It was a three-storey building, overshadowed by great mansions on either side. There was a square double gate leading to the courtyard, and this, with its great iron bars and nails, would have needed a battering-ram to force it if it were locked against you. There was only one small window on the ground-floor, and it was protected by bars. Most of the Strand houses were well defended like this, for they stood outside the City walls and the protection of the watch. When I say that three hundred criminals are hanged in London every year, you'll see the need for bolts and bars.

'You'll never get in there,' said Kit.

I was inclined to agree. I raised my eyes to the upper windows. Each storey projected a couple of feet beyond the one below, so that the house hung over the narrow lane like a crag. If it had been a crag, I might have managed something. As it was, the smooth cream plaster offered no holds.

'Perhaps there's a back way,' I suggested.

'I doubt it. I think these houses all go straight up from the river. Of course, there might be a water-gate, if we got a boat . . .'

We turned down an alley, hoping it might bring us to another lane at the back of the house. But, as we had feared, it was a dead end. It brought us to a flight of seaweedy stairs, leading straight down into the grey Thames. Standing on these steps, we could look a hundred yards along the curved river and see the house of the yellow gentleman, unmistakable between its taller neighbours, rising sheer from the water. As we watched, an upper casement was flung back and the head and shoulders of a servant appeared with a bucket, the contents of which he sent slopping down.

'No bars on that window,' I said.

'But no landing-stage or steps or anything,' Kit pointed out. Nearly all the bigger houses had their entrance from the river as well, because it was the pleasantest highway between Westminster and the far side of London.

I looked at the house with narrow eyes. The noonday sun was shining full on it, and every irregularity and crevice stood out in black shadow. There was a lot of timbering on this side . . .

'I could get up to that window,' I said at last. 'I'd need a boat and . . . let me see . . . say, half a dozen daggers.'

'Half a dozen *what*?'

'Daggers. I could stick them into the beams where there's no other hold. I think we could borrow half a dozen, don't you?'

Kit began to look alarmed now my plan was really taking shape; but I soon reassured her, and she promised to do her share.

We timed the burglary for twilight, when there would be less risk of being noticed by people passing up and down the river, but sufficient light remaining for me to see what I was doing inside the house. There was no sense in going at midnight if it meant candles. Also, the tide would be well up about eight o'clock, shortening my climb.

We booked the boat for seven. The waterman was a little dubious about our youth, but I soon convinced him that I knew how to manage the craft. We told him we were going to row up past Westminster, and drift back by moonlight with the current and the ebb-tide. He wished us a pleasant trip . . .

We collected the daggers at the theatre, as well as a length of rope which I thought might be handy for the return journey down the face of the house. As soon as the performance was over, we made for the Strand. Kit carried a bundle of girl's clothes, borrowed from the company's wardrobe, and changed into them in the fields near Lincoln's Inn. Her job was to watch the landward side of the house. In girl's clothes she would arouse less suspicion, and, if the yellow gentleman looked out, he would not be reminded of the boy he had seen that morning. Finally, as a girl, she would be better fitted to play the part required of her.

Which was . . . ?

Well, you'll have been thinking, no doubt, that the most difficult part of our problem was still unsolved: what would the yellow gentleman and the other inmates of the house be doing all the time I ransacked their belongings?

Kit volunteered to look after them. I didn't like dragging her into danger, but she went haughty at once.

'There's no danger for me – I'm an *actor*. I can do this on my head. Pete,' she added accusingly, 'you're doing what you swore you wouldn't – treating me as a girl!'

'Sorry,' I said. 'All right, then. Remember: when the clocks stop striking eight, that's the moment for you to act.'

'Good luck,' she answered, 'and do be careful.'

I went away to get the boat. The sun was setting behind Westminster Abbey, and the incoming tide stung my nostrils with the tang of the sea.

I took the oars and swung the boat out on the brimming surface of the river.

12.

Treason on Thames-side

I can tell you, the lowest window looked mighty high from the boat in which I sat – and I had decided rather to try the upper windows, since there was less risk of anyone being in the bedrooms at this time of the evening.

Luckily, heights don't trouble me. I've scrambled about on too many crags at home, when below me there was sickening space, followed by hard rock, instead of water to break my fall.

It had been a quarter to eight when I took the boat out. Now, as I groped in the gloom for something to tie it to, the time must have been only a few minutes short of the hour. The water slap-slapped against the wall. As I stood up, the boat creaked and echoed woodenly. Far up-river a party of diners-out sang lustily as their boat zigzagged towards Westminster. Their torches streamed redly in the green twilight. Anyone who happened to be scanning the Thames at that moment was far more likely to be watching the revellers than noticing the shadowy figure under the wall.

There was nothing to which I could tie my boat, so it was lucky I had brought all the daggers I could lay hands on. I drove one into a wooden pillar which stood out from the stone foundation wall. It didn't go in very far: the wood was tough. I pulled it out and tried again, using more force. This time it seemed firmly embedded, I knotted the painter of the boat round its crossed handle, and prepared to climb.

The first ten feet were the worst. There were no holds, and I had to use daggers, thrust into the timber with all my force. It isn't easy to drive a dagger into hard timber, especially when you are standing on another dagger and precariously holding on by your left hand to a third. Each time I put my weight on a fresh dagger my heart went into my mouth and I nerved myself for the splash below. Each time I lifted my foot from the lowest dagger, I felt the wildest exultation of relief.

Soon it got easier. There were beams, projecting three or four inches from the smooth plaster, and offering handy ledges for finger-tips and toes. Above my head, but a little to the left, there was an open window. I decided to peep through very cautiously, and, if the

room was empty, to take a chance and swing my leg over the sill. The clocks would be striking the hour at any moment now, and that meant that Kit would put her share of the plan into execution. Once she started there wouldn't be any time to waste.

I was out of luck. The room wasn't empty. I could hear men's voices as I climbed higher. After all, I should have to use the top-floor windows.

'Well, I don't intend to lose *my* head on Tower Hill,' came the voice of the yellow gentleman, so suddenly and so crystal-clear that I almost let go my hold. 'Oh,

I know others have said that before me, and they've gone to the scaffold none the less. But it's different this time.'

'My dear fellow,' interposed a mild, mocking voice, 'it always is different.'

I shifted my position slightly and listened intently. Anxious as I was to stop playing the fly on the wall, I thought this conversation too interesting to miss. Luckily, I had got a place where I could relax a little and remain, if need be, for several minutes without moving.

'I wish I could tell you more of the details,' said the yellow gentleman irritably, 'then you wouldn't croak like an old frog. Anyhow, you know Morton.'

'Morton?'The unseen friend sounded as surprised as I was. 'You mean Philip Morton? Is he in this?'

'Up to his ears!'

There was silence for a moment. Then the other voice said in a new tone: 'If Morton's in it, it *is* different. There's something unearthly about that young man. I remember when he first came to Whitehall, she took one look at him and said to Essex, "The Devil's come to Court!" And she gave him about as cordial a welcome.'

'I know,' the yellow gentleman agreed. 'He's never forgiven her.'

All the clocks in the City began to strike. I flattened myself against the house, ready for action. The two voices went on in tranquil discussion, but I could gather no more than I had already guessed, that something like high treason was being plotted in that room, and that Sir Philip Morton, that bad penny of my life, seemed to be mixed up in it.

Bang! Bang!

Far away, at the other side of the house, Kit was hammering madly on the street door. From where I was I could hear it only dimly.

'What the deuce is that?' said the yellow gentleman.

'Someone knocking,' answered the other, like a fool.

'But *who*?' I could guess they were feeling rather nervous. When you have a guilty secret, a sudden knocking on doors can be very upsetting. 'I'll see,' said the yellow gentleman, and I heard his chair grate back and the door of the room open. He called downstairs – I could hear nothing distinctly – and then he must have turned to address his companion.

'Some girl, they say. Attacked by a cutpurse in the lane outside – came screaming and hammering on our gate. Let's go down, shall we?'

'By all means. Is it all right to leave . . . these?'

'Oh, goodness, yes. There's nothing there that would hang a dog.'

'Then let's go down and comfort the distressed damsel.'

The door closed behind them, and in a couple of seconds my leg was over the window-sill.

It was a small room. My eyes took in a tall cupboard, a couple of chairs, stools, a chest, a table bearing wine, candles (unlit), and a heap of books and papers. I could have whooped when I saw my play-script, half-hidden by what looked in the gloom like letters and household accounts.

Perhaps I should have acted differently – bundled together as much of that litter as I could stuff into my doublet, or at any rate carried some to the window and tried to read it. True, the yellow gentleman had assured his friend that there was nothing incriminating, but I fancy I might have learnt some names, at least, which would have proved helpful afterwards and saved me from some of the misfortunes which befell me.

But there, I wasn't an experienced Government agent then, and it wasn't second-nature to me to do these things. I was a boy with his heart in his mouth, scared that at any moment the yellow gentleman might come back – perhaps to fetch the wine from the table to revive the 'distressed damsel'. I'd got what I'd come for, and I wasn't stopping. I went through the window with the heavy wad of paper bulging my doublet, and let myself down with infinite care.

Going down was at least as bad as going up. I had to dangle my feet in the gathering darkness, swinging this way and that till I felt the foothold. When I got to my stairway of daggers, I had to pull them out after me, one by one, as I went down. It took a strong tug to bring them out of the timber, and I had to be careful lest the force I exerted should topple me from my precarious hold. As I drew them forth, I stuck them in my belt till I looked like a pirate – or should have done, had it been light enough to look like anything.

The most awkward part was getting back into the boat, which had swung round on its painter and (as usual with boats when you leave them) wasn't at all where I had left it, or where I wanted. Still, I didn't worry by that time; I was safe enough now, even if I got a wetting. Actually, I avoided even that, and managed to step dry-shod into the boat after all. As I did so, one of the daggers slipped from my belt and plopped into the water with a mighty splash. That was a pity, I thought, and would cost me the price of a new one, but it was better than leaving the tell-tale weapon in the wall.

'. . . Only a water-rat, I expect,' came the yellow

gentleman's voice, and to my dismay I saw his head far above me, dark against a glow of candle-light, peering down from the window. 'No! there's a boat down there!'

I still hadn't untied the boat, and I knew that, what with unshipping the oars and everything, it would take me a minute or two to get outside pistol range.

Better to disarm suspicion . . . I knew that the boat showed only dimly from the window above, and that I myself was visible only as a vague shape. That shape might just as well be two people huddled close as one.

'Darling!' I said in my huskiest, deepest voice.

'Dearest!' I answered, with a little feminine giggle. And then, in a tone of alarm: 'Oh, *Robbie*, someone's *looking*!'

'Be off with you!' the yellow gentleman shouted. 'You can't tie up there; do your billing and cooing somewhere else, not under our windows!' His voice faded as he turned back into the room. 'Only a pair of love-sick idiots . . .'

I hurriedly got out the oars and sculled away.

By the time I had restored the boat to its owner, and gone to our agreed meeting-place at Temple Bar, Kit was waiting for me, still in her girl's clothes.

'Got it!' I said triumphantly. And then: 'What are

you giggling about?' Kit was positively bubbling, like a kettle just ready to boil over.

'I – fooled them so – so *beautifully!*' she managed to get out. 'They sent a servant with me to see me safely inside the gates. They were so considerate – it was really a shame. They gave me wine to revive me.'

'I suppose that's why you're giggling like a child of eight,' I said, taking her arm. She needed it.

It was late when we got home to our lodgings. I lit a candle hurriedly, while Kit looked round for some food. I wanted to assure myself that the play-script was intact.

Yes, it was complete. There was only one thing which puzzled me. In the middle of the play, in a long speech by the Chorus, there was one sentence underlined:

> *the nimble gunner*
> *With linstock now the devilish cannon touches,*
> *And down goes all before them!*

I knew that I hadn't marked those lines. The only man who would be likely to underline them would be the man in charge of the stage effects, and he, of course, had his own copy. It was a trivial, meaningless mystery, but it bothered me. I drew Kit's attention to it, but she could explain it no better than I.

'And what's this?' she asked, turning the bundle of script and pointing to a few scribbled lines on the back. 'Have you been composing poetry in your spare time? Plenty of Crossing out, anyhow!'

I stared at the black, unfamiliar writing. Allowing for the numerous corrections, the verses ran:

> *Since words and wit are weak in friendship's need,*
> *Even to say a tithe of that I would,*
> *Now bend a penetrating eye and read,*
> *Divining how I'd greet thee if I could.*
> *No golden voice have I to sing thy praise;*
> *Eloquence is not mine; I lack the tongue*
> *Worthy to celebrate these happy days,*
> *Singing their glory as it should be sung.*

It was a sonnet – and a pretty poor one, I thought. The second half went:

> *But 'tis the meaning matters, not the form;*
> *Y-wis, the thought behind is more than face.*
> *Proserpina herself is not more warm,*
> *Even when dusky Pluto's fond embrace*
> *Enfolds her, than these wishes that I send,*
> *Love-charged, to hail the birthday of my friend.*

Underneath was scribbled '26 copies' and a tick, as though the copies had been duly made.

'Silly stuff,' I said. 'I'd be ashamed to write it. It doesn't mean anything.'

'On the contrary,' retorted Kit, 'I think it means a great deal. The question is, what exactly? More treason, if I know anything!'

13.

The Clue of the Sonnet

There was something odd about that poem, certainly.

'I smell a rat,' I said.

'So do I,' Kit agreed – 'a rat that's been dead a long, long time.'

Think it out for yourself. On the face of it, there was nothing suspicious about the poem. When I was a boy – more, perhaps, than nowadays – it was quite a usual thing for a man to toss off a sonnet, as easily as he would write a letter, and send it to his friend as a form of birthday greeting, or congratulation on his marriage, or something of that sort. Some of the sonnets might be good as poetry, if a man like Shakespeare wrote them, or they mightn't be worth the notepaper they were written on.

Now, it doesn't take an expert to see that the yellow gentleman's composition (supposing it was his) was no great shakes at poetry. If you read it again, you'll see that it spends most of its fourteen lines saying 'Words fail me' in a rambling and roundabout fashion.

'If he felt he couldn't express his feelings properly,' said Kit, 'why did he try to make a poem?'

'And have twenty-six copies written out?' I added in amazement, remembering the impositions at school and what hard work they were.

'False modesty! Perhaps he really think's he's written a masterpiece.'

'The bit about Proserpina and Pluto is very bad,' I said critically. When you worked every day with a man like Shakespeare you did learn the meaning of good verse, if nothing else.

'Yes,' Kit agreed. 'Pluto's the King of the Underworld, a pale, cold land of shadows. I should think his embrace must be a chilly sort of business! Certainly, if I wanted a nice poetic comparison for warmth, I'd think of something better. The sun, say, or a fire.'

I felt sure it wasn't a genuine birthday greeting. The poem was written with some other motive, and the writer hadn't cared a farthing about sense or style. There was a hidden meaning wrapped up in it somewhere: he'd concentrated his mind on that.

'Listen,' I said, reading:

> *'Now bend a penetrative eye and read,*
> *Divining how I'd greet thee if I could.*

Isn't that as plain as a pikestaff? He's warning the reader to read between the lines.'

'And farther on,' cried Kit excitedly:

> *'But 'tis the meaning matters, not the form . . .'*

'"Y-wis",' I said. 'What in Heaven's name is the meaning of "y-wis"?'

She wrinkled her brow, trying to remember. 'I've met the word somewhere before . . . let's see . . . I believe it was in a poem by Spenser. I think it means "truly" or "certainly".'

'That would make sense, anyhow. But what a word!'

'I s'pose he thought it sounded grand and poetical.'

'Twenty-six copies,' I murmured. 'For whom? Twenty-six conspirators?'

Kit said she wouldn't be surprised. Nor – I thought – after the conversation I had overheard, should I.

Well, we pored over that poem till our candle guttered out – which didn't seem to matter, because we knew every word by heart. But could we get the secret meaning out of it? Not a glimmer!

Afterwards, of course, we realized that it had been staring us in the face all the time, and we cursed ourselves for fools, because we hadn't seen what was under our very noses. We'd been warm on the scent, had we but known it, when we talked of that silly word 'y-wis', and wondered why the writer had used it. If we'd thought a little harder, everything would have come crystal-clear; but there, we didn't . . . Once the light went out, all chance of unravelling the mystery that night went with it; but, of course, we hadn't an inkling of that, and sat on in the dark, cudgelling our brains to no purpose whatever.

I wonder if it really *was* so obvious? Once we'd been shown, it looked so easy. Well, have another glance at the sonnet yourself before I give the game away, and just see if you would have done better than we did.

What were we to do?

We couldn't just let the matter rest because we hadn't been able to solve the puzzle ourselves. We knew enough to feel certain that we had stumbled on the fringe of a big mystery, and that the proper authorities ought to be informed.

Should we take Shakespeare into our confidence? I was shy of doing that, for it would mean confessing what a fool I had been with my copy of his play.

Should we go off by ourselves and call on the City

Sheriff? Would he believe our story – with no more convincing evidence than a scribbled sonnet which didn't read quite right? I had an unpleasant suspicion that the criticism of poetry was possibly not the Sheriff's strongest point. And who were *we*, anyhow? Two of those rascally young actors who impudently set up their stages just outside the City boundary, whence they could thumb their noses at the Sheriff and Mayor and the rest of the authorities!

'A boot to our backsides – that's all we'll get, most likely,' said Kit pessimistically.

'Or awkward questions about ourselves – who we are, and where we come from. Neither of us wants that particularly.'

'We'll have to chance it, though. If those men really said what you say they did –'

'Of course! Do you think I dreamt it?'

'This is something big, something we daren't keep to ourselves.'

'I know,' I said quickly. 'I've had an idea. Sir Joseph Mompesson!'

'Sir Joseph Momp –; but, Pete, he's a Secretary of State; he's such a *big* man –'

'We want a big man,' I retorted. 'You said yourself this thing is big. Sir Joseph is a Cumberland man, that's the point. He was born at New Hall in the blessed shadow of Skiddaw itself. He went to our school.' I grinned at a memory. How sick of Sir Joseph's name we boys used to get! He was the master's favourite, shining example. If I had heard it once, I had heard twenty times the story of Joe Mompesson who went up to the Queen's College at Oxford, took his degrees, went abroad, became a master of foreign languages, and then came to Court and started a brilliant career in the Queen's service. Well, now I was going to benefit by that past boredom.

'First thing tomorrow,' I said, 'we're going to find his house and call on him. He won't refuse to see an old schoolfellow, even if we weren't at Keswick together.'

And so – a little to my surprise and relief – it proved.

We were lucky in finding Sir Joseph at home and disengaged. When I sent in my true name, and said I was a late scholar of the same school, we weren't kept waiting a minute.

Sir Joseph was sitting before a blazing fire of sea-coal, for the day was chilly. His long face, lolling against the high chair-back, was as warm and merry as the dancing flames.

'Brownrigg? Brownrigg? Come in, boys. The very name's like a whiff of peat-smoke! And what's the news from Cumberland? Have you brought me any sweet butter?'

'I – I'm afraid not, sir,' I said. 'It's – it's rather a long time since we left Cumberland. If we'd known you –'

'There, there,' he said quickly, seeing that I was crestfallen. 'Only my fun! I have a cook who can make sweet butter that you'd swear came from the dales. You shall taste some in a minute. Sit you down, sit you down. How's Keswick, and Crosthwaite, and Threlkeld, and all the other places? What a devil of a journey it is! Yet if I weren't tied to Court I'd make it often enough.'

It was quite hard to tell him our business, he was so eager to question us about home. But at last I managed to get to my story, and he heard me to the end in silence. Then he said:

'You're not romancing, my lad?'

'No, sir.' I showed him the script and the sonnet written on the back of the last sheet. He read it with pursed lips.

'Bad,' he said. Then his eyes twinkled. 'But no worse than scores of us have written when we've been young and in love. You can't chop a man's head off for writing bad poetry.'

'It's a pity,' said Kit, who had kept mum, mostly.

'I'll tell you what I'll do,' said Sir Joseph after a moment's meditation. 'I can't make head or tail of this, but I know who can – if there is anything in it. I'll send this manuscript to him. Don't look worried; we shan't let Mr Shakespeare's play fall into wrong hands again. It'll be as safe with us as a State document. In fact, if your idea about a code is correct, it soon *will* be a State document.'

'Will you want to see us again?' I asked.

'Oh, most certainly. You'll have to repeat this story of yours, on oath maybe, and sign a deposition. Can you meet me again tonight?'

'Yes, sir; we're free as soon as the play's over.'

'Seven o'clock will be soon enough. In the meantime, not a whisper to anyone – not so much as a mouse's squeak. Understand?'

'Yes, sir.'

Sir Joseph sat tugging at his ear. 'Not at this house,' he said finally. 'At Sir Robert Cecil's. Anyone will direct you. It's the big new brick-and-timber house in the Strand – you'll notice the fine smooth pavement in front of it. Ask for Sir Robert. And, Brownrigg –'

'Yes, sir?'

'Walk warily till then. Look behind you. Take care of yourselves.'

I was glad of his warning. It showed he was taking us seriously. There was probably no danger, for, in the welter of papers on the yellow gentleman's table, the absence of the play-script might go unnoticed for some time, long enough for him to feel uncertain when and where he had mislaid it. It looked, too, as though he might have finished with it – the twenty-six copies of the sonnet had evidently been made – and in that case the yellow gentleman would not trouble himself unduly.

'Anyhow,' I reassured Kit as we walked away from Sir Joseph's, 'the yellow gentleman doesn't even know that I know where he lives, and there's no earthly reason why he should connect me with the distressed damsel he comforted last night *or* the courting couple in the boat.'

None the less, I wasn't sorry when the day passed without incident. You hear of strange things in London. Men die in the dark alleys, and the murderers are often untraced. In the mountains a man's cry will bring other men running for a mile, but in London the death-scream is only another sound to be swallowed up in the din of the shopkeepers and hawkers, the tumult of traffic and the clamour of the bells. A body may lie in the gutter for half an hour before someone is inquisitive enough to turn it over – its owner is so much more likely to be drunk than dead. I took Sir Joseph's advice and looked behind us, for I'd no fancy to wear a dagger between my shoulders.

Seven struck as we knocked on Sir Robert Cecil's door. We were evidently expected. Before I had half finished stammering our names and business we were swept inside and ushered up staircases and along passages into a panelled room. Sir Joseph was warming himself – or trying to warm himself – at a poor little fire under an immense chimney. 'These are the boys,' he said cheerfully.

Sir Robert Cecil looked at us gravely across his table.

He was a quiet man, not at all imposing – very ordinary, you would say. He was dressed entirely in black, save for his starched white ruff. I knew that he was the son of the great Lord Burghley, and I knew that he himself was someone important, someone very near the Queen. I did not know till afterwards that he was the head of her Secret Service.

He stirred a little in his chair and sighed. He did not stand up the whole time we were there, and I should never have guessed that he was deformed, almost a hunch-back.

'*Another* plot?' he said wearily.

'That remains to be seen,' said Sir Joseph. 'Hear young Brownrigg's story from his own lips.'

So I told it again. I described the yellow gentleman in detail, and the house. Kit added a few further details.

Sir Robert sharpened one quill after another with a tiny silver-handled knife, and laid them methodically on his inkstand. At last he broke silence.

'Your yellow gentleman is Sir David Vicars,' he said dryly. 'We have had our suspicions for some time.'

Kit shot a triumphant glance at me. I winked back, and then saw that Sir Joseph had seen me, and began to flush, until he winked too. He was standing behind Sir Robert's chair, so he could pull all the faces he liked.

'Morton?' went on Sir Robert. 'That is rather more of a surprise. You heard no other names, I suppose?'

'No, sir; I'm sorry, sir.'

'Morton, Cumberland. Vicars, Northumberland. H'm!' Sir Robert twisted in his chair and smiled wryly at Sir Joseph. 'A disloyal lot, in the North, Mompesson!'

'Dash it, I'm Cumberland myself! So are these boys! There's good and bad up yonder, the same as everywhere else.'

'Oh yes. Oh yes.' Sir Robert reached for a quill and played with it, turning the white feather over and over against the black table-top. 'But after all, Mompesson, the last serious rebellion *was* the Rising of the North.'

'That was twenty-five years ago – longer.'

'All the same, I have a fancy that not all the northern gentlemen have learnt their lesson. And now these boys come along with their story of Sir Philip Morton. The North again! Coincidence, you think? Possibly. Yet if we could only know the names of the twenty-six gentlemen who are receiving copies of that sonnet, I think we should see a good collection of fine old northern families.'

'Have you found out what it means?' asked Sir Joseph hurriedly, not much liking the way the talk had turned.

'I sent it to my cousin Francis. He has his uses. He has the knack of these things. He should be here by now. Unless it's too hard a nut for him to crack.'

But apparently it wasn't, for a couple of minutes later there was a discreet tap on the door and a gentleman walked in with a package under his arm, wrapped up in a piece of dark velvet.

'Well, Francis?'

'It was quite easy,' said the newcomer, undoing his package and laying my play-script on the table. 'One of the easiest codes in existence. I should have thought you'd have seen it yourself at a glance.'

'I *have* other things to do,' Sir Robert suggested mildly. 'Why was it so obvious?'

'That word "y-wis", for instance –' Sir Francis Bacon laid a neat forefinger on the line. 'Why did he use that particular word when he could have said "truly"?'

'The Devil alone knows,' said Sir Robert. 'I'm no poet.'

Sir Francis snorted. He looked round at us all with an air of pleased superiority. He had cold, clever eyes, like a snake. 'Because, gentlemen, he wanted to begin that line with a letter Y. He had to. And there aren't a lot of words which begin with Y – and still fewer which fit the rhythm and sense of his poem. It's a childish cipher. You, boy,' he said, motioning me forward to the table, 'read Sir Robert his hidden message.'

'But –' I began, and then, in a moment, I saw. You simply read down the sonnet taking the initial letters of each line. SENDNEWSBYPEEL. 'Send news by peel,' I said.

'There you are,' said Sir Francis.

'And may I ask what in Heaven's name it *means*?' said Sir Robert.

'Yes,' said Sir Joseph. 'How much forrader are we? "Send news by peel." What do you make of that, Sir Francis?'

'Oh, quite simple, quite simple. For some reason the conspirators are getting nervous. They want to communicate in a more secret manner; no doubt there are reports to make, letters to exchange –'

'Yes, yes; but this peel?'

'That's a well-known method of transmitting

messages. A tiny cut in the peel of an orange, say – slip in a small folded paper, send a basket of oranges to your friend, and there you are.'

'What about the juice?' I said, and he stared at me very haughtily as if I'd no right to speak except when he told me.

'Yes, wouldn't it make the ink run?' queried Sir Robert.

'Possibly an apple would be better, Robert. If you like, I'll test the idea myself.'

'I can't see it will help matters very much,' said his cousin, playing with his quill. 'Of course, we can have some of these suspected gentry watched, though' – he sighed – 'spies are so expensive. If we're to find out every time a man receives a gift of fruit, it will need a small army of our agents planted in their various households. I don't quite see how it can be done. Sir Philip Morton, for instance, has gone home to Cumberland. How are we to get a spy into *his* house?'

There was an awkward silence. Sir Joseph Mompesson was the first to break it. 'Haven't you enough evidence to arrest some of these fellows now? This Vicars, say, whom our young friend so aptly calls "the yellow gentleman".'

'I could do that,' admitted Sir Robert, 'but I prefer to leave them all at liberty till we know the names of the others.'

'He could be questioned.'

'I dislike . . . questioning,' said Sir Robert, with a faint shudder of distaste. 'The results are unreliable. Men say anything on the rack: they're as apt to accuse the innocent as the guilty. It's better to watch and watch till you know everything, and then – pounce.'

'I've another idea about this "peel",' said Sir Francis. 'It might refer to bells, of course – a peal of bells.'*

They discussed that for five minutes, but it didn't help matters much. One *can* send news by bell – news of a great victory or the death of a monarch or something like that – but it was hard to see how conspirators could use such a very public means of communication.

Suddenly, as I stood there kicking my heels, listening to their argument, I had an inspiration.

'I know, sir!'

They all looked at me – Sir Francis scornful, Sir Joseph encouraging, Sir Robert just . . . well, like a mask. His lips moved as he twiddled his pen. 'Speak up, boy.'

'Mightn't it be one of the peels in Cumberland – maybe Sir Philip Morton's?'

Sir Robert looked blanker than ever. But Sir Joseph slapped his wide breeches and swore.

* Spelling was slacker in those days, and one might write of a 'peel of bells'.

'The boy's got it! And I a Cumberland man – but so long away from home that dashed if I thought of it!'

Sir Robert tapped the table. 'Please explain.'

'Peel-towers –' Sir Joseph and I began together, and we told Sir Robert what they were, and how Sir Philip Morton certainly had one, though it was supposed to be shut up now and uninhabited.

'An ideal headquarters for a plot,' said Sir Joseph. 'I'll be bound that's what it means. They're to send all news by way of the peel-tower. Plain as the nose on my face.'

Sir Robert digested the new theory. The white quill turned over and over against the blackened oak of his table, and it seemed years before his thin lips moved.

'It's worth investigation. Someone will have to go to Cumberland.'

He raised his eyes and looked straight at me.

14.

Secret Agents

That was how I joined the Secret Service of the Queen.

It was a service unknown, I suppose, to ninety-nine out of a hundred ordinary folks. They saw, or more likely heard of, Queen Elizabeth mingling freely with her subjects – sitting in church, leading the dances, riding the countryside, stopping to speak to Tom, Dick, or Harry, as the mood took her. They knew there were plenty of men who would gladly see Bess dead. They knew there had been attempt after attempt upon her life, and yet by a miracle (as they supposed) she lived.

It wasn't such a miracle.

Bess wouldn't take care of herself, she took the wildest risks, but she had faithful servants to take care of her. First Walsingham, who'd died a few years before I came to London, then Robert Cecil. It was Walsingham who built up a wonderful system of Government spies and agents, to ferret out all the plots that were going and scotch them before they got too dangerous. Walsingham's men were everywhere. They knew all the codes, all the tricks of the trade. One conspiracy after another reared its head – and Walsingham, selecting just the right moment, sliced off that head, sometimes on Tower Hill, sometimes elsewhere.

Robert Cecil took over the organization which he left. He grumbled at the expense, paid off a number of agents, but kept the thing in being. There didn't seem so much risk now. One by one the Queen's most dangerous enemies were dying off, and she herself wouldn't live for ever. It was easier now to wait for Nature to remove her, instead of risking one's own neck to hasten the process by poison or pistol bullet. But Robert Cecil was a careful man, and he still kept his eyes open, in case . . . It was lucky he did so.

All this, and a good deal more, we learnt as we rode northwards with Tom Boyd.

We'd been introduced to him one day, soon after that memorable evening at Sir Robert's. A shabby little man he seemed, with a bald forehead and very few teeth – the sort of man you'd never remember having seen before. I suppose that was one reason why he made such a good agent.

'So you're my guides, are you?' he said, with a chuckle, and his West Country voice was as rich and thick as cream. He gripped our hands, and we were friends at once.

Sir Robert had decided, after a good deal of pentwiddling, to send one of his best agents to have a sniff round Cumberland. But he had no suitable man who knew the country. If Tom Boyd went alone, he would be as helpless in the mountains as a blind man; and in the villages, talking to folk in that Somerset voice of his, he'd be as noticeable as a Negro.

So it was agreed that I should go with him. If the key to the mystery lay in the Morton country, I knew all those hills and dales like the knuckles of my own hand. People would talk to me as a neighbour, and they'd talk to Boyd if I was there to vouch for him.

'But if I'm recognized,' I pointed out, 'I'll be in trouble at once with Sir Philip's men. Couldn't I have a free pardon or something, so they can't touch me?'

Sir Robert had shaken his head at that. 'You can't have a pardon till you've been convicted of a crime. We can promise you this, though: if you are unfortunate and get arrested, we'll see that nothing unpleasant happens to you.' He smiled. 'Even we Secretaries of State have to observe the formalities of the law.'

'I'll keep him out of mischief, sir,' promised Boyd.

'My plan's this: we go up to Cumberland disguised as a pedlar and his boy. When we get on the ground, we find ourselves a hiding-place; maybe young Brownrigg knows a barn where we can sleep, or perhaps his dad will shelter us. Young Brownrigg doesn't show his nose by daylight, unless it's dead safe. Only his family and trusted friends know that he's back home at all. If he can put me in touch with them, I can manage all the rest.'

Of course, Kit wanted to come, and of course nobody except myself saw any necessity for a second boy to go on the expedition. What they'd have said if they'd known the truth about her, goodness alone knows!

So there was a great argument, and ninety-nine reasons quoted against her going, and the end of it was (as you can imagine) that when we rode out along the Great North Road with our little string of packhorses there were three of us, not two.

It was early in June now, and the weather the best you could wish for. Our way took us up the eastern side of England, through country which was entirely new to us. We touched the fringe of Sherwood Forest, I remember, and slept a night on the close-cropped greensward under the great oaks which must have stood there since Robin's day. Then we went on across the Vale of York, which was flat as a board and very dull to our eyes, being hill-people. This road went on and on to the borders of Scotland, but we were glad when it was time to turn off towards Richmond, and follow one of the lonely trails up over the Yorkshire mountains and down the other side into our home country.

It was good to be in the high hills again, though these Yorkshire fells are different from ours, being mostly green and rounded, without sharp crags or precipices. But they *were* mountains. We could see the heather, though it wasn't yet in bloom. Wherever we went we could hear the friendly sound of water, leaping down over the square grey stones. Of stone, too, were the houses, like those of home; we'd left behind us the red brick and straw thatch, the white plaster and tarred beams. People's voices were more friendly, and they looked at us with the light of welcome in their faces, being lonely folk in their high valleys. The food was *food* again, not just something to stay your hunger with.

We really traded as we went along: we had a fine mixed store of ribbons and Sheffield knives, salt and spice, liquorice and Spanish oranges, song-sheets, and about everything else you can think of.

'No harm in a profitable sideline,' said Tom. 'We agents aren't paid too well, and I'm getting on. Some day I'll be too old for this game, and what then? I've got to save. I fancy a little tavern of my own, not too far from the Tower.' He laughed. 'I might name it "At the Sign of the Keyhole", eh?'

So on we went up the valleys, wasting no time, but trading enough for people to think us genuine. Then, one morning I'll never forget, we started at dawn, left the last farmstead behind, and climbed up and up the soaring spine of the mountains. We looked to the priming of our pistols. There were wild men up here, working in the mines and living like beasts. Back in the dale villages they'd told us fearsome tales of pedlars who'd been murdered for the few shillings in their purses, and then thrown down bottomless pits in the limestone, so that their bodies were never found. We kept a sharp look out, I can tell you, but no one interfered with us.

It's not for that I remember the morning, but for the blessed moment when we topped the last crest of the trail and saw a whole new world laid out at our feet.

Right and left marched the fells on which we stood, ridge after ridge, summit after summit, from the Trent almost to the Tyne. Before us spread the Vale of Eden, wide, green, and gracious, dotted with little grey towns and villages, dappled with grey cloud-shadows, slowly drifting across the green and gold of the sunny land.

And beyond the Vale, a day's journey, with their proud peaks stabbing through a layer of white cloud, rose the mountains of home . . . Skiddaw and Scafell,

Blencathra and Glaramara, Helvellyn and Great Gable, like giants in their glory. You'll say I couldn't see all those, and I couldn't tell one from another at so great a distance. I'll tell you: I almost persuaded myself I could see my own home, nestling under the shoulder of our own mountain!

All Tom said was: 'Now we're coming into your own country, lads, we'd better think of disguising you a bit. Not a full disguise, mind, but just something to distract people's attention from your ordinary appearance. It's always the peculiarity that folks notice. If you've a patch on your eye or an ugly scar on your cheek, that's how they'll think of you and remember you.'

We agreed that, for the time being, I should have my head swathed in bandages, and pretend I'd been thrown from my horse. It was a hot kind of disguise for June, but I hoped I wouldn't need to wear it for longer than a day or two.

'What about Kit?' said Tom. 'I can't have you *both* bandaged.'

'I'm disguised enough as I am for Cumberland,' said she, and told him, straight out, what we knew we shouldn't be able to hide from him much longer.

'Well, I'm hanged!' he said, and looked at her with his big mouth open, showing his few lonely teeth. 'If I'd have known –'

'You can't send me back now,' said Kit quickly.

'She's proved herself on the trip up,' I pointed out. 'No boy could have done better.'

'And a girl might be useful in some ways – *as* a girl. Pete's going to borrow one of his sister's dresses for me, and then, if need be, I can turn into a girl again, as I did that night we went to the yellow gentleman's house. Pete couldn't have managed without me then.'

'All right, all right,' said Tom, with a dazed grin; 'but if I was your father, wouldn't I wallop you when I got you home?'

'Would you?' she said very quietly, looking straight at him.

He shook his head. 'I'd as soon try to wallop a tigress,' he admitted. 'I pity Sir Philip; he doesn't know what he's up against. There's only one thing.'

'What's that?'

'He ought to thank his lucky stars you won't marry him. Better a quick death on Tower Hill than a lifetime with you.'

'I *do* think you're rude,' she complained.

Kit was guide that day. East Cumberland was her country. She'd been born by the banks of Ullswater, and when she came of age, she said, she'd inherit land there. Her guardian lived over towards Shap more, and that was a spot we gave a wide berth. When she was younger she must have ranged the fells like a mountain cat: she knew every hill, every waterfall, every little tarn lying in the lap of the moor.

We slept that night near the lower end of Ullswater. Kit pointed up the long thin lake, black and yellow under the full moon.'I've a house up there,'she boasted, 'with glass in the windows and tapestry with pictures on the wall. And land – ooh, acres and acres. All mine when I'm older. That's what sneaky Philip wanted. To join the estates and buy more – or steal them, and be lord of the land from Penrith to Keswick.'

'We'll put a spoke in his wheel,' I said.

The next morning I took the leadership of our little cavalcade, and we groped our way westwards, by lonely byways, across the hump of moor which lies between Ullswater and the Skiddaw country. We had avoided Penrith deliberately. We wanted to get to our true work, and if we went where there were too many people the trading delayed us. So, before the sun had climbed high behind us, round the side of Great Mell we came, and there across the low ground, pale and grey in the full flood of the morning light, rose Blencathra, my own mountain, my home.

Those last few miles passed with maddening slowness. When we reached my own valley it became especially unwise to hurry. Every house we called at, and I had to bend my red face over the goods, to hide it from neighbours who had known me from the cradle. Luckily, Tom did most of the talking, and Kit chipped in when it was necessary, so I never had to open my mouth except once to grunt, 'Fell off my horse!' when kindly Mrs Bell asked about my bandages.

It was afternoon when we rode splashing through the beck and looked up the grass slope to the low grey house couched under the mountain.

'Mind that washing!' called my mother sharply, bustling out and shading her eyes at us. It was all laid out, white and spotless, on the close turf, with stones holding it down. Mother looked down at us as though we were all strangers, but she smiled at the sight of our great bundles. She loved to pick over a pedlar's stock; it was one of her few pleasures, living so far from markets and being so busy.

'Good day to you,' she said to Tom as he swung himself from the saddle. 'And what have you brought to show me? All the silks of China and the perfumes of Arabia?'

'Something more precious, ma'am,' said Tom, with a smile and a bow, and I ran forward to her, grinning from ear to ear.

I needn't describe the next hour. You know what mothers are, and maybe you know or you can imagine how it feels to come home after nearly a year away.

'But I don't think you should have come home, all the same,' she said, looking worried. 'I don't know what your dad will say when he comes in. Glad as we all are to see you, and your friends! But' – she shook her head – 'it's dangerous.'

I told her then – Tom nodding his permission – that I was now in the Queen's service. Sir Philip was more likely to see the inside of a prison than ever I was.

'All the same,' she said, 'you won't want him to know you're back in these parts, or it may upset Mr Boyd's plans.' She knitted her brow in thought. 'We can trust most of the neighbours, but not all. Here and there you find there's a man trying to make up to Sir Philip. People tell tales.' She turned to Tom with a gesture of apology. 'We'd gladly take you all in, Mr Boyd, and hide you if we could, but I just don't think it's possible. It would leak out that you were here. It isn't that *we'd* mind, but it wouldn't help you in your work.'

'I quite understand, Mrs Brownrigg.'

'Since Peter threw that rock,' said my mother, smiling, 'this house has got itself a reputation – and it's not one the family is ashamed of. All the same –'

'That's all right. We'll find somewhere.'

'I know!' I cried. 'We'll go and live at the Stronghold!'

15.

The Lonely Tower

'This'll suit us down to the ground,' said Tom cheerily. 'Comfortable? Goodness, man, when you've slept in stuffy cupboards and hidden up to your neck in a river and stowed away for a hundred miles in a boat full of rotting fish – *then* you know the meaning of luxury.'

'Well,' said Dad doubtfully, 'if there's anything you find you want, just send down to the farm after dark. We'll none of us come near you unless you send word for us.'

'It'll be safer that way, Mr Brownrigg.'

'Good night, Dad,' I said.

'Good night, Peter. Good night, lass. 'Night, Mr Boyd.' My father picked up his stick and stepped away, a shadow on the moonlit mountainside.

The Stronghold made a splendid hiding-place. The overhanging boulder offered ample shelter. When it was light we would gather bracken and make comfortable beds with the blankets we had brought. There was good drinking water within a stone's throw, and, as I have told you, Sir Philip's peel-tower was only a little way down the valley. By walking half a mile we could reach a spot from which we could look right down on it.

We could get all the food we wanted by sending someone after dark to my mother. Our horses were stabled at Bell's farm, ready for us if we needed them in a hurry. That was safer than keeping them at ours. Mr Bell owned more horses, anyhow, and he had a story ready to account for these if necessary. Everything had been done very carefully; it had been a lot of trouble, but it hadn't been worth taking risks. First we had ridden out of Lonsdale in full view of everyone as if leaving the district; then Mr Bell had met us in the dusk on the main road and taken over the horses; finally, my father had joined us and helped us carry our gear up the mountain before the moon rose.

We snatched some sleep, in spite of our excitement and the hardness of the ground. Then, when the sun got up, I led the way cautiously along the mountainside.

There stood the old tower, black and lonely against the morning. Not a wisp of smoke curled from the roof.

'A very nice place for a little dirty work,' said Tom slowly as he looked down on it. He took something from his doublet, a kind of metal tube with glass in it, and put it to his eye. Then he handed it to me. I looked through and gasped softly. It was like magic – the tower seemed much nearer. I could see the front door quite plainly at the head of the stone stairs.

'What on earth –?' I began.

'It's called a perspective glass. I don't suppose you've ever seen one before? Very useful on work like this.'

It would have been, no doubt, if there had been

anything to see. But the peel stood there looking as empty and forlorn as a hollow tree.

For the first hour Kit and I insisted on staying there, though Tom urged us to go back to the camp, where we could talk freely and move about.

'Watching's a dull job,' he warned us. 'We shall have to divide it up into shifts, so many hours each. No sense in us all lying here the whole time.'

After an hour, when the novelty had worn off and we had tired of his perspective glass, we agreed with him and went off, promising to relieve him later. We went to a place where I knew we should find plenty of bracken, and began to gather bundles for our beds.

'We shall look well,' I said gloomily, 'if my whole idea was wrong and we've come up here on a wild-goose chase.'

'You're in such a dashed hurry,' Kit complained. 'Did you expect to see Philip come straight out of the door in a mask or something?'

'That door doesn't look as if it's been opened for years.'

'Wait and see. Even if we're wrong about the peel, we can go and watch Philip's new house. We know he's up to something.'

Between us, we watched that tower until sunset, and not a soul did we see. Kit began to get dispirited too. Only

Tom remained in perfect good-humour; he'd enjoyed his lazy day, he said, after so much travelling.

'This game is like fishing,' he said. 'You want a good deal of patience.' He filled his pipe and puffed away with great enjoyment. 'There's nobody there now, but it doesn't say that nobody *comes*. They may wait till darkness. I'm going back in a few minutes.'

'You won't be able to see anything,' Kit objected – 'anyhow, till moonrise.'

'No, but I can hear. You two get some sleep now.'

He woke us at dawn. As soon as I opened my eyes I asked if anything had happened.

'Not a thing,' he said cheerfully. 'There's nobody there.'

'What do we do now?'

'Go down and see if there *has* been anyone lately.'

We went down the grey mountainside in silence. It was a dank morning, with swathes of mist waist-high and a tiny sort of rain which beaded softly on our woollen clothes. The peel loomed above us. It was queer: it had seemed so small and boxlike when we looked down from the mountain, and now, when we stood at the foot of its greasy-wet steps, it soared skywards like the tower of Babel.

There wasn't a sound. Not a dog barking, not a voice. The old fortress waited for us in the dawn as if we were its first visitors for centuries. None the less, something made my hand tighten round the pistol I carried in the breast of my doublet.

Tom marched straight up the steps and hammered on the door. I was taken aback by this unexpected action. I stepped in front of Kit and tried to feel ready for anything.

There was no answer to the knocking. Tom tried the door, peered at the lock as though he were shortsighted, and came down the steps with a smile.

'Why did you knock?' I asked.

'Oh, just in case. There was one chance in a hundred that someone was there after all. If so, he'd have seen and heard us, and wondered what we were up to. So I had a fine story all ready about being lost.'

'You look mighty pleased with yourself,' said Kit.

'I am. That door has been used recently.'

I asked how he knew.

'Fresh oil in the lock. Mud on the steps – and these steps must be scoured clean by a real driving storm. Horses have been here within the last day or two. They were tethered to that iron ring. See the hoof-marks? See how the rust's been rubbed off the ring? They had their nose-bags, too – look, there's a little corn the birds haven't found yet. I should think there were men here the day before yesterday.'

'And now, I s'pose, no one'll come near the place again for another month,' I prophesied. Still, I was encouraged to have even this slight confirmation of my theory.

We prowled round for some minutes without finding anything else of interest. I wished we could get inside. The others were thinking the same.

'That door would keep out an army,' said Kit.

'If there was someone inside to shoot the bolts,' Tom corrected her. 'If the place is empty, there's only the lock. I might be able to pick that. Let's have a look.'

We all went up the steps and stood round the big lock. Tom began to tinker with it, singing low under his breath. It was wonderful the number of odd tools he carried about with him; he used to call them, jokingly, his portable torture-chamber.

'I think I can manage this,' he murmured cheerfully.

It was just then I heard the dull echo of horses' hooves, thrown back by the abrupt wall of the mountain.

'Someone's coming!' I hissed.

We dropped over the side of the steps without waiting to go down properly. Luckily, there was tall bracken within fifty yards. We flashed across the open ground like rabbits. Looking back, I knew we couldn't have been seen yet. The riders were still hidden in a dip.

'Keep dead still,' Tom told us. 'Heads down. I'll do all the peeping.'

But from where I lay it was perfectly easy to look through a screen of feathery bracken-fronds without being seen.

I could hear voices now, and the jingle of harness. Then there rode into view, first Sir Philip, on his familiar grey gelding, then two other men, and finally, on a glossy, beautiful chestnut, our old friend, the yellow gentleman.

They reined in at the foot of the steps, and Sir Philip pointed to the tethering-ring. So the other three were visiting the place for the first time? The previous visitors must have been other conspirators.

When they had unlocked the door and gone inside, Tom wriggled closer to me. 'You know the lie of the land,' he whispered. 'Need we stay here in the wet? Can we get away without risk? They might happen to look out of the windows.'

'Follow me,' I grunted. I led them on a fine scramble, first through the dripping bracken and then up the deep-worn gully which carries the stream from our tarn down to the Glendermakin. They were both quite surprised when we suddenly emerged beside the little lake, on the very threshold of our camp.

'Food!' said Tom bluntly, and no one challenged the proposal. We sat down, glad that the sun was starting to break through and dry our soaked clothes.

'Morton and Vicars,' said Tom. 'Did you know either of the others?'

I shook my head.

'One looked familiar to me,' said Kit, after some hesitation. 'I've seen him with Sir Philip. I think he lives over in Borrowdale, but I can't remember his name.'

'Never mind; we'll find out. When we've eaten, we'll make some notes. Describe the men, what they wore, what their horses were like. Then, if need be, we can ask round – Peter's father might know, or that Mr Bell. Every detail helps.'

No one felt tired or bored now. The hunt had started. As soon as we'd eaten and made our notes, we hurried back to our vantage-point along the mountainside, and trained the perspective glass on the peel.

The horses were still there, stamping and flicking at flies. After a while, two other men appeared, one with a hawk on his fist, as if to provide a natural excuse for his rovings. They dismounted and went inside. We couldn't identify either of them, but they didn't look as though they had ridden far that morning.

'We'll track them down,' Tom muttered.

Within half an hour three more men appeared, on foot and from a different direction. They came swinging down the steep flank of Souther Fell. There was one with a broad black beard like a spade.

'Anthony Duncan,' I said. 'He's a biggish landowner from Troutbeck way, just over yonder.' I rolled over on my elbow and stared at Tom. 'What *are* they up to, all of them?'

'That's what we're here to find out.'

There were several other arrivals later, some mounted, some on foot. The latter had probably left their horses in a convenient place a mile or two away, and taken short cuts over the rough ground. If the whole gathering had ridden up the same bridle-path it might have been noticed.

The last arrival we all three recognized with grunts of surprise. He was a well-known Cumberland nobleman – I won't mention his name, for he's been dead these many years and there is no sense in reviving the disgrace for his family. When he'd jingled up the steps and vanished into the doorway, Tom said between his teeth:

'This is getting bigger and uglier.'

We tried to tempt him, but he wouldn't say much. Only: 'If it's what I'm *afraid* it is, we've got to work quickly – more quickly than I thought. It's a matter of life or death, and not just one life, but many. What wouldn't I give to hear what they're discussing now!'

But there wasn't the remotest chance of repeating my Thames-side escapade. There was someone watching on the roof of the tower; we caught a glimpse of his plumed hat at intervals. No one would get near the place without his seeing them.

It was lucky we were so high on the mountain, so that we could withdraw when we wanted to. We did so about noon. Tom said there was no sense in grilling there in the sun any longer; we'd learnt all we could just by watching, and our next move would have to be different.

'Couldn't we get inside the tower when they've gone?' I suggested. 'It's possible they keep papers hidden there.'

'That's what I'm reckoning,' he said, puffing at his tobacco. 'I want to get as many names as possible – at once. If those fellows go away all right, I'm going into the tower to look round.' He caught our questioning glances and said: 'Yes, alone. Sorry to disappoint you, but this is too important to study personal feelings. I can concentrate better if I'm alone. I want to go in and out of that place without leaving a sign that I've been there. Three people treble the risk. Besides, I want Peter to keep watch on the bridle-path. Someone might take it into his head to come back . . .'

'Can I watch with Peter?' Kit asked in a small voice.

'I'd rather you didn't. Two don't watch better than one: each distracts the other. You stay in camp.'

We didn't argue. We were under orders now. We knew how much depended on the success of Tom's work, and we realized he was right. Two sentries tend to whisper together and take their eyes off the country. Alone, you've nothing to think of but the job.

As a consolation for Kit, Tom asked her to keep watch during the afternoon, while he got some sleep. I went along to relieve her about five o'clock. Most of the conspirators had gone hours ago, she said, but there were still two horses tethered outside. I sent her back to the Stronghold. As soon as the last man went, I would run back to Tom and tell him the coast was clear.

But it was quite late in the evening before Sir Philip and the yellow gentleman came out, closing the door behind them. For safety's sake I didn't stir till they had ridden well down the valley. Then I ran to the Stronghold, where I found them eating supper.

'I was just coming to relieve you,' said Tom.

'They've gone at last. What a time they've been!'

'I imagine they've some mighty extensive prepara-
tions to make,' he muttered. He yawned and stretched
himself. 'Have some food quickly, and we'll be getting
down.'

'Let's go now,' I offered; 'it's almost dark as it is.'

'No hurry. It'll be dark already inside, with those little
slits of windows. I'll take a stub of candle.'

While I ate, he outlined his plan. I was to walk well
down the valley and squat beside the bridle-path. At the
first sign of anyone approaching, I was to give a warning
signal, an owl hoot, and then clear out of the danger
zone, repeating the hoot a time or two to make sure that
Tom heard it. He in turn, if he finished his work without
interruption, was to whistle. This would tell me that my
duty was over, and I could make my way back to camp.
Kit was to stay there throughout the proceedings.

'And let's hope there's no real owl in the district!'
said Tom.

'Shall I whistle instead?'

'No. A whistle gives the show away. Only whistle
when there's no one else to hear. I'll tell you what,
though – if you do hear a real owl, whistle to let me
know it *wasn't* you. I hope that won't muddle you?'

'Oh no. Owl-hoot for danger, whistle for all clear.'

'I shan't sleep a wink,' Kit complained. 'I shall be
listening to all the strange noises in the valley!'

I swallowed my last mouthful, Tom tapped out his pipe, and we went. We scarcely whispered as we moved down the hill. Soon we stood at the foot of the steps again, and the peel blotted out a great oblong of star-speckled sky. Tom groped for my hand, just squeezed it encouragingly, and mounted the steps. I would have given a lot to stay, but I knew my job. I turned away and tramped down the bridle-path.

When I had gone about half a mile I judged it was far enough, and stopped. If I signalled danger a minute or two before it reached me, Tom should have ample time to fix the door and make his escape. If I went too far down the path, the signals might not carry between us. What wind there was, I noticed, was in my face. That was good. It would help me to hear anyone coming, and it would carry my signal to Tom.

I settled down to listen. The Glendermakin made a great to-do, boiling and bubbling over its stony bed, but I soon got used to it. The river didn't count any more. I counted the night as silent, because my mind stopped registering a sound which was so continuous and unchanging. But I knew that a voice, a hoof-beat, or the jingle of a bridle, would strike my ear as distinctly as a pistol shot.

How long would Tom be? He had warned me to prepare for a lengthy vigil. He might have to search the tower from top to bottom – certainly would do, if he didn't find what he wanted more easily. The chances of the whole affair being a complete failure were, he said, at least two to one. Spies spent most of their time drawing blank, and in time I should get used to his plodding methods.

I thought of many things as I sat there on a convenient flat rock, my ears cocked for the least fresh sound.

Of my comfortable bed over the mountain at Lonsdale . . . Of our London friends, fat Desmond and his kindly wife, just starting on another summer tour, hot-tempered Burbage and serene Shakespeare . . . The new play would be in full rehearsal now; in a week they were due to perform it at Court. That was the one thing Kit and I had regretted about leaving London on this expedition. We had wanted to act in *Henry the Fifth* . . . Then I thought of Sir Robert Cecil, waiting patiently for the reports which Tom was to send him by courier, twiddling his white quill pen as he planned and organized and dovetailed our work with that of other secret agents . . . And my mind wandered on to Sir Joseph Mompesson, and how he would like to be sitting here with me for an hour, with a cold Cumberland rock striking through his baggy breeches and the dawn waiting behind the eastern fells.

What was that? A whistle! No. Imagination. Funny tricks it plays after you've been alone for some time.

The moon was riding high. I moved down the path a few yards to a bend which gave me a view for a mile down the valley. Little risk of being caught napping now. I should see anyone coming as clearly as I should in daylight.

What a long time Tom was! He must have been hours. He was probably copying numbers of documents by candlelight. I knew he didn't intend to steal the originals if he could help it. He didn't want to arouse the suspicions of the plotters until Cecil was ready to pounce on the whole brood.

It would soon be dawn. The wind was stronger than ever in my face. It whined up the valley, stretching the grasses taut, bending the bracken. I realized that if Tom signalled now I should never hear him. The wind would snatch the sound from his lips and whip it away in the opposite direction. It was quite likely that this had already happened sometime ago, or it might even be that the whistle I thought I had fancied had been real after all. Tom was probably now snug in the Stronghold telling Kit all about it, and wondering why I was so long making my way back.

I waited till the moon had paled to a mere glimmer and the dawn was on tiptoe behind the hill. Then, knowing that I could still, by backward glances, keep watch on the path nearly all the way back to camp, I judged that I might fairly leave my post.

Kit rose from the rocks to greet me as I neared our hiding-place. She looked white and anxious.

'I was getting frightened,' she said.

'I'm safe and sound,' I assured her. 'Has Tom come back?'

'No. I haven't seen him. Haven't you?'

'No.'

Neither of us ever saw him again.

16.

The Heart of the Secret

We went along the mountain. The tower looked as deserted as ever. We scanned the fellside eagerly. There was no sign of Tom trudging home.

What had happened? He couldn't still be there, surely – not of choice, at any rate. But he might have fallen into some trap. A door might have clicked behind him, making him a prisoner in some windowless room unable to signal to us. Or there might have been one of those cupboards with a hidden spring, which send a poisoned spike into the unwary hand which sets it off. We had both heard a great deal of such Italian villainies. Sir Philip was capable of anything.

'We must find out – if we can possibly get inside,' said Kit.

'I'll go,' I said. I was in command for the moment. I'd have given a lot for Kit's company, but I knew I wasn't justified in taking her. 'You keep watch here, and – can you whistle?'

'Of course I can whistle!' she said scornfully.

Tom had once told us that, if anything ever happened to him, we were to go to the nearest sheriff or magistrate, and get him to send word, by official courier, to Robert Cecil. But the present business might be so urgent that this wouldn't be sufficient. We must allow two or three days for the message to reach London, and as long again (or longer) for fresh instructions and another of Cecil's men to arrive in Cumberland. Could we afford to stand still and do nothing for so long?

'You keep watch,' I repeated. 'If I don't come out of that building within twenty minutes –'

'I'm coming in to look for you!'

'Oh no, you're not, my girl. You're going to race over the mountain and find my dad. Tell him all you know, and he'll do something. If necessary, he'll get a band of men and they'll break into the tower.'

'Let's both go and do that now.'

'Not likely. Tom may be all right. Or he may have fallen downstairs and knocked himself out. I'll be careful, never fear. I won't touch anything. And I'll feel every board before I put my weight on it. I've got a pistol.'

'What use is a *pistol*, if there's no one there?'

I laughed and touched the brass butt where it stuck out from my doublet. 'It's a comfort, anyway,' I said. And I went snaking down the fellside, just in case anyone was watching. But I didn't get the feeling that anyone was.

I ran up the stone steps on silent tiptoe. The door stood inches open. That saved me a job, anyhow, and a job I wasn't sure I could have managed without Tom's handy little tools. He must be still inside. He'd never have left the door like that.

I pushed it back cautiously and slipped inside, still holding it with my left hand while my right closed over my pistol. There was no sound from the door. He who had oiled the lock had also attended to the hinges, and the massive timber swung silently at my push. I stood still for a whole minute, listening intently and letting my eyes get used to the dimness. The windows were small and high. Shafts of sunlight slanted through them and revealed that the room was empty except for spiders' webs and a broken stool.

The floor was solid, flagged with grey slabs. All the same, I took no chances. Instead of crossing straight to the doorway of the inner room, I crept round by way of the three walls. The other room was like the first, but in one corner, built into the thickness of the outside wall, there was a spiral staircase. It led down into the pitch darkness of the ground-floor, which in these peel-towers is always used as a cellar and store-house. It also continued upwards to the second floor, where the bedrooms were in the days when the peel was inhabited.

It was darkish over in this corner, but I could see a patch of something at the foot of the stairs. It was wet. Water, I told myself but I wondered . . . I bent down gingerly and poked the tip of my finger into it then straightened myself and raised my hand to the light. If it was water, there'd be nothing to see except a wet shininess on my skin.

It wasn't water. I knew that as soon as I felt the stickiness. Then I saw, on my finger-tip, a neat oval of red so dark that it was almost black.

One is used to the sight of blood. I've seen plenty of sheep killed. I've watched bear-baiting and bull-baiting and cock-fights and all the sports that we Englishmen love. But for a moment, as I stared at the dark sticki-ness on my own finger, I felt sick.

I pulled myself together. Perhaps Tom had merely had an accident – slipped on those tricky, twisting stairs as I'd suggested to Kit. Then, where was he? Perhaps dazed and confused, he'd staggered on down the stairs into the cellar, and fainted there. Well, it wouldn't take

long to see. If he was unconscious, I'd have to get Kit
to help me up with him.

I felt my way stair by stair, down into the gloom of
the store-cellar. One, two, three, four . . . At each step
I paused and listened. I wished I had a candle.

As my foot flattened silently on the fifth stair, I heard
something.

Footsteps overhead, coming down from the upper
storey. For a deluded moment I almost shouted 'Tom!'
but it was well I didn't. For there were two men, and
they were talking.

I stood where I was, my pistol cocked. Were they
coming all the way down? No, apparently. They had
stopped in that inner room which had once been
the parlour. Crouching five stairs down, I could hear
plainly.

'I hope he *was* alone,' said a gruff voice.

'Getting frightened, Anthony?' The second voice was
high and mocking. I guessed that the first speaker was
Anthony Duncan of Troutbeck, he of the black beard.
How had he got here without our knowing? Then I
realized what had happened. We had never taken an
exact count of the men leaving the tower. We had seen
some depart on foot, and we had seen the last of the
horses ridden away, and we hadn't allowed for one or
two men staying behind.

'I'm not frightened,' growled Duncan, 'but it gives you a shock. I should have thought this place was safe enough. Lucky Philip's groom spotted him.'

'Lucky the man was using one of those glasses,' said his companion, with a laugh. 'Useful things – but they *do* catch the sunlight.'

'I wonder how he got on to the place. I hope he hadn't talked to anyone else. I don't like it, James. We thought we were all right here –'

'Don't worry, my dear Anthony. We'll see what Philip says. We can easily change our headquarters.'

'The time's getting so near now. Couldn't we act sooner? It's this waiting.'

'No; it must be the twenty-ninth. That's the day we know for certain we can deal with Bess.'

I could hear Duncan clearing his throat. He said hesitantly. 'Do you know . . . exactly . . . how it's to be done?'

'Why, yes! Don't you? It was Vicar's notion in the first place . . .'

I listened, stiff and taut on the dark stairway, as the full horror of the conspiracy was revealed.

Tom had been right. This thing was getting bigger, bigger and uglier.

The Queen was to be murdered – that we had suspected all along. She was to die in the middle of the command performance of Shakespeare's play.

It had all been thought out in devilish detail. The conspirators had looked for an opportunity – not a sudden chance, but some definite occasion that could be foreseen. *Henry the Fifth* offered the perfect opportunity: a date fixed weeks beforehand; the Queen seated in her chair, with no one between her and the stage; an expert pistol-shot hidden in the curtains not twenty paces away . . .

'The man's name is John Somers,' said the lazy voice above me.

I started. John Somers! I knew him. He was one of Burbage's company, a disappointed, disgruntled player of third-rate parts. I had often heard him boast of his marksmanship. He was just the kind of man to lend himself to a piece of dirty work such as this. And, of course, he'd be able to stand behind the stage curtains without any question.

'Lucky to find such a man in the company,' Duncan was saying.

'Oh, most actors will do anything if it's made worth their while. Or course, he's scared for his skin afterwards, but we persuaded him. He'll fire his shot just at the moment when there's a terrific row of stage cannon. If people hear the shot, they'll think it's part of the play.'

The blood rushed to my cheeks. Of course! Those lines, faintly under-scored in the stolen copy of the play:

> *. . . the nimble gunner*
> *With linstock now the devilish cannon touches,*
> *And down goes all before them!*

I could hear and see it all in my imagination. The Queen sitting there in her jewels, her great skirts spread like a peacock's tail; the speaker of the Chorus declaiming his lines; the splendid roar of cannon on which our manager prided himself; the faint snap of the pistol; the Queen twitching in her seat, then slowly nodding forward as though she felt sleepy, while blood gradually soaked through to her stiff outer bodice, and made a dark patch spread wider and wider round the bullet-hole . . .

'H'm,' said Duncan. 'He counts on enough time to slip away?'

The other man's cold chuckle was more brutal than the most ferocious threat.

'He *counts* on it,' he drawled. 'But Philip and I thought better not. Julian Nesby will be in attendance on the Queen. He's to jump on the stage and run the fellow through. That'll save awkward questions.'

'More blood,' said Duncan, and I could tell the shudder in his voice. He wasn't a bad man, Anthony Duncan, but weak and ambitious.

'Of course. That's only the beginning.'

I couldn't follow the rest of their plans with the same clearness, because Duncan knew them as well as his friend. So, instead of listening to a straightforward description, I had to piece together odd hints and guess, half the time, what they referred to.

Of the main plan there was no shadow of doubt. On the day fixed for the Queen's assassination there was to be an uprising in the northern counties. Simultaneously, a Spanish fleet was to cross the Bay of Biscay from Ferrol, and – not repeating the mistake of the Great Armada – make an immediate landing at Falmouth.

The high politics behind all this I couldn't pretend to grasp. I couldn't tell from their talk even whom they meant to set upon the throne of England. But one thing I realized without any telling: Sir Philip Morton and his friends were going to be the big men in the new order. Sir Philip had outgrown such petty methods of stealing common lands and marrying heiresses. He was playing for the highest stakes.

It was just then I heard, faint but clear, Kit's whistle.

So did the two men. 'What's that?' said Duncan with

the harshness of fear in his voice. I heard him turn on his heel and stride away. In a few moments he was back. 'All right,' he growled. 'Must have been that groom –'

'Philip's man?'

'Yes; he's riding up the valley.'

'Philip said he'd come back himself this morning. He must have been hindered.'

Again came that whistle, piercing and urgent now. It was bitterly funny, in a way. Poor Kit was desperately warning me against the one man who was riding up the valley; yet I was already besieged, unknowingly, by the pair inside the tower. She whistled a third time. She must be frantic. I knew how I'd have felt in her place. But I couldn't answer her.

I had to make a quick decision.

Should I make a dash for it? I could shoot one of the men point-blank, and, with any luck, get out of the room before the other got over his surprise. That would mean a desperate chase up the mountain, with at least one man close on my heels, and the groom not far behind.

Or should I feel my way silently downstairs into the cellar in the hope of remaining there undiscovered? Was there any reason why the men should come down there? I knew there was one very probable reason: Tom's body might be lying there, and they might decide to remove it.

On the whole, though, the second course seemed the wiser. I would go down and crouch in the darkness. If they didn't come near me, well and good. If they *did* – well, I should still have my pistol. There was a sporting chance of taking them by surprise and fighting my way out.

The cellar, which a little while before had yawned like a well of horror, became suddenly a haven of refuge. I turned and took another step down.

There must have been blood on the stair. My foot slithered over the edge. I went headlong. The pistol leapt from the breast of my doublet, bounced away, and went off with a tremendous bang. My head struck the curving wall with a resounding crash, and that was the last I knew for a considerable time.

17.

Held for Questioning

In my ears was the ceaseless murmur of water. There was the fresh smell of water too. Do you think water has no smell? Horses know better. Stand by the lakeside with your eyes shut and you will never doubt that it is water which spreads in front of you.

My head ached dully. My knuckles smarted where I had dashed the skin from them. It was some moments before I felt any inclination to sit up and open my eyes.

I was sitting on a sloping shelf of grass, in front of a tumbledown stone hovel. The grass ended in a grey shingle. Then the water stretched, grey and sullen under the clouds, for a quarter of a mile or more. There was a boat, with one man in it, making for the other side, where dense woods rose steeply from the lake. The fells behind them were blotted out by low-hanging mist. As I watched, the man disappeared into an inlet, and for an instant I imagined I was now utterly alone.

'So you've come to your senses?' growled a deep voice, and there was Anthony Duncan towering above me. I didn't answer immediately, so he went on, not unkindly: 'That was a nasty crack you gave yourself, but you'll be all right.'

'Where am I?' I asked. It's what people always ask when they come round in such circumstances, but when the view in front of you is unfamiliar, it seems the most sensible question.

'Never you mind. Safe enough.'

I didn't feel particularly safe, though I was glad to be with Duncan, rather than the cold-blooded man I had heard talking with him in the peel. I glanced behind me. There was the old hut, moss-covered, with heather growing between its stones and a rotten door hanging crazily on its hinges. There was no sound of anyone inside. There were a couple of sycamores behind the hut, and farther back I caught a glimpse of the top branches of other trees.

'Like a drink?' asked Duncan.

'Please.'

He went over to a basket, took out a pewter mug, and walked slowly down to the water's edge. I watched him with half-closed eyes, shamming faint. This was my chance. I felt sure he had no companions near, and if I got twenty yards start it would take a nimbler man than Duncan to overtake me. Once I got up the fellside, the low mists would help me, and, though they would make it harder for me to get my bearings and find where I was, that was a minor point. The main thing was to escape.

I waited till Duncan reached the shingle and stooped. I heard him grunt and his legs crack: he was a stiff-jointed rheumaticky man. I could have shouted with joy at the sound of those creaking knees. I was as good as free.

I bunched my muscles ready. His puffed breeches were most temptingly curved against the grey water. Had I been near enough, one hefty kick would have sent him flying into the lake. Instead, I sprang to my feet and tore round the side of the hut. If he had a pistol, he had no time to use it. I went bounding up a little knoll, covered with trees and bracken, and as I went I realized how much my fall had taken out of me. My legs were weak, I reeled and stumbled, but sheer will-power carried me up the hillock.

'Come back, you fool!' bellowed Duncan.

I ran on, ducking through bushes. I could see water ahead, shining through the leaves. I turned left. Water again. Duncan was pounding along behind me. I rushed to the right, and still I saw the steel-grey lake in front of me. By now the truth had dawned on me – we were on a tiny islet in the middle.

There was nothing left but to swim for it. There was no place to dive from; the island at this point was fringed with jagged rocks, sprinkled in shallow water. I started to wade and scramble towards the open water, but Duncan reached me before I was knee-deep. He seized me like a bear and carried me back, breathless but struggling, and threw me down on the grass.

'Little fool,' he said. 'Do you want to be tethered like an old goat?'

He dragged me back to the hut. In the food-basket was a length of cord ready for the purpose. He tied my ankles together; then, without cutting the cord, my wrists as well. At first he was going to fasten them behind my back, but he relented. 'You'll need to eat,' he said, and tied my hands in front, with enough rope to raise them to my mouth and thus, in a clumsy way, feed myself. There was a loaf in the basket, some meat, and other things, including a small glass bottle of wine. He cut a slab of bread and a slice of the meat, and shoved them into my coupled hands.

'You'll have to manage as best you can. I'm not trusting you with a knife. Come on; you might as well eat. We may have a long wait.'

'Wait for what?' I asked sullenly. I bent my head and raised my hands, and started to gnaw the food. I needed it.

'Never you mind. You'll see soon enough.'

We didn't speak again for a few minutes. I was thinking hard. I had guessed where we were. Since we certainly weren't on Derwentwater, we were probably on one of the small islets in the uppermost reach of Ullswater some miles from the peel. But why had they taken the trouble to carry me here and leave me under guard? For whom or what were we waiting?

Luckily, Duncan was even more curious than I was, and after one or two sidelong glances he could keep quiet no longer.

'What were you doing there?' he demanded roughly. 'How much do you know?' I could see that, big man as he was, he was secretly afraid.

'Quite a lot,' I answered. I wasn't sure how to handle the situation, but my impulse was to play on his fear and keep him guessing.

'Anyone else know? Except that other man?'

That was awkward. I didn't want to stir up suspicions which might lead them on Kit's trail, or to my home. Still, it might be dangerous to let him think I was alone. There would be a strong temptation then to silence me for good and all, as I felt sure by now they had silenced poor Tom.

'You'll know soon enough,' I said.

His face twitched. 'Yes,' he agreed. 'We'll know all right

– when Sir Philip comes. You'll talk to him. He knows how to make people talk. I'm trying to save you from that.' He took a long drink from the wine-bottle, as if he had thoughts he wanted to forget. Then he turned to me earnestly, wiping his hand across his black beard. 'We've got to know, lad. Our lives depend on it. You can't blame us. But I don't want you to be hurt. I know who you are, and I know your family. I don't want to start any feud. I want you to look on me as your friend.'

'You're my jailer,' I retorted.

'And lucky for you I am!'

'Why?'

'The others aren't so soft-hearted. Talk to *me*, lad, before the others come. Then I swear I won't let them touch you.'

'I know what to expect from them, once I've talked. A knife in the ribs, my clothes stuffed with stones, and a grave at the bottom of the lake!'

'No,' he protested.

'What then?'

'You'll be kept here on this island till everything's started. It's only a week, after all. We shan't care what you do then. It'll be too late to matter.'

I looked at him stubbornly. 'I wish I could trust your friends as well as I'd trust you, Mr Duncan. But I can't. I shan't talk yet.'

He made a gesture of impatience. I knew he was desperately worried for his own sake. The conspirators must be feeling very frightened today. First Tom, then me . . . They must all be wondering if there were any more of us. Clearly, they no longer felt safe in the peel, or they would have kept me there, instead of bundling me off, at such risk and inconvenience to themselves, across country to this island.

Yes, I must keep them on tenterhooks. They wouldn't kill me so long as there was a chance of my confessing how much I knew. Once I'd talked, I should be safer dead. I must hold my knowledge like the very breath of life inside me. On the other hand, suppose they tortured me . . . ? The old fear came back in all its horror.

Duncan picked up the wine. It was getting low. He half-raised the bottle to his lips, then shoved it into my hands. 'You can finish this,' he grunted. 'Warm you up. Don't want to get chilled.'

There was sense in that. After the knock I'd had it was best to keep warm. Though it was June, the day had turned out cold and sunless; the way the clouds were piling up, it looked stormy. I suspected, though, that Duncan had another motive apart from good nature. He imagined that the wine might loosen my tongue, as I was only a boy.

'Go on, drink up,' he bade me. 'I'll see if I can get a fire going.'

I raised the bottle obediently, gripping it carefully between my bound hands, and gulped at the bitter warming liquor. Duncan moved away, grunting under his breath as he gathered sticks. Gradually his search took him zigzagging round the islet. There wasn't much fuel to be found.

I clasped the bottle in my fingers. It was the nearest thing to a weapon within reach; but what use was it to me, seated on the ground, unable to rise? I glanced round me again. Could I drop it into a hiding-place for possible use if I ever got my hands free? No; Duncan would be sure to miss it.

What a fool I was! I held in my hands now the very means of getting them free. The question was, would he hear? And was there time to do it before he came back with his armful of fuel?

No harm in taking the chance. I leant towards the wall of the hut and dashed the bottle against the stone with all the force I could achieve. The wine splashed my legs as the glass flew into fragments. It hadn't made much noise.

I bent forward and searched the grass for a suitable fragment. It was fortunate that the bottle had been thin – the pieces were razor-sharp. I managed to get a big triangular piece in the fingers of my right hand.

Now the trouble was that, twist as I would, I could not bring the glass into contact with the cord round my wrists. What I could do, though, was to bend forward and saw at the cord round my ankles, and after half a minute of frenzied work the last strand gave and my legs at least were free.

What now? I couldn't swim with my hands bound. I couldn't fight Duncan with my feet. I seemed no nearer to freedom.

Duncan was coming back, his arms full of brushwood. I kept my feet together, with the loose cords still wrapped round them, and prayed that he would notice nothing. He seemed intent on the sky.

'Blowing up for a storm all right,' he said. 'Best get the fire going inside and be all cosy.'

'Ye-es,' I muttered drowsily. 'I feel like a sleep. It was that wine.'

He nodded and smiled. Then he ducked his head and went into the doorway. I heard him drop the wood on the hearth and grope for flint and steel.

There was a handy-sized stone in the grass some yards away. Now, with my feet free, it was no longer out of reach . . .

I didn't want to hurt Duncan. He'd been as kind to

me as a man could, considering that we were enemies. If he'd been crueller, more ruthless, he would never have given me the chance to hurt him.

But I couldn't be squeamish. I'd no doubt that Duncan had helped, however unwillingly, to murder Tom. He was a traitor, ready to plunge the whole countryside into civil war for the sake of his own ambitions.

Besides, it wasn't at all certain that I was going to succeed. He was a big man, and I a boy with bound hands. David and Goliath. And if I failed – if I merely hurt him without disabling him – he wasn't going to be kind to me any more.

I lifted the stone in my hands and the insects scurried over the damp patch beneath it. I walked shakily to the door of the hut and peeped in. If Duncan was facing the door, I should have to wait and catch him as he came out. But my luck was in again. He was kneeling with his back to me, building up sticks on the hearth in the centre of the hut, but not three paces away.

I stepped in silently, raised my arms above my head, and brought them down. There was no sound but that of the blow and the dry snapping of wood as he pitched forward across the hearth. I backed into the open air, feeling fainter and sicker than I had for a long time. A drop of rain splashed on my cheek. I shivered and pulled myself together with an effort.

First, my hands. Now that I could move about freely, it wasn't so difficult. Duncan, no doubt, had a knife somewhere, but for the moment I didn't feel like going into the dark hut again. I contrived to wedge a piece of glass upright in the ground, held between my feet, and so, after several irritating failures, fray the cord sufficiently to break it.

Before I had finished there was a loud clap of thunder, and a great wind came rushing down the lake, driving rain before it as sharp as pike-points, and churning the water into waves like the sea.

I saw that my luck had changed in the very moment of my triumph. No swimmer could face the quarter-mile crossing in a storm like that. I was still a prisoner.

18.

Striding Edge

The woods were blotted out in an instant. The wind roared like twenty thousand devils and the rain hissed on land and lake. I dived into the shelter of the doorway.

Ullswater, I'd often heard, was specially liable to sudden squalls like this, and while they raged no boatman, let alone a swimmer, would venture out. The storm was apt to gather over the Kirkstone Pass and then come rolling down, irresistible as a charge of cavalry. The lake is long and narrow, a deep trough hemmed by great mountains like Helvellyn and the High Street. The storms rush down it, rumbling and roaring against the fells on either side.

There were two sources of consolation: it was likely to blow over quickly and, if I couldn't leave the island, no more could anyone else reach it.

Meanwhile, there was Duncan to think of.

I crept nearer to him and listened. The rain was drumming on the roof and hissing through the central hole which served as a chimney. The wind wailed and at intervals the thunder crashed. It was no wonder that, for some moments, I could not be sure that I had heard him breathing.

But he was. The deep, sobbing breath of an unconscious man. I was glad I hadn't killed him.

I rolled him over and loosened the ruff at his throat. I wanted him to be comfortable, but I daren't take any chances. To be on the safe side, I skipped out into the storm and brought in the pieces of cord. I tied his wrists and ankles as he had tied mine, but I made a very firm resolve that he should not escape as I had done. I took away his sword and searched for a dagger or pistol, but could find no trace of any other weapon. The cords were soaking wet, and it struck me that in time they would shrink and tighten, cutting into the flesh. If he was still unconscious when I left him, I must slacken them.

By the time I had finished with my captive, the wind had dropped considerably and the rain was coming only in gusty showers, with longer intervals after each. The lake was no longer whipped into white horses of foam, and by degrees the woodlands were coming into view again, at first as colourless masses, but soon as bright green foliage, with bands of watery sunlight straying across them. I judged the time to be early evening. It had been a full day!

Better not stay any longer . . . I had never felt less like a quarter-mile swim, but it was better than waiting for Sir Philip's arrival. There was a heavy swell on the lake, but I thought I could manage it.

I stripped off my doublet and long hose – I needed all possible freedom – and sank them with stones where they would not be noticed easily. My shoes I laced on my hip, for I couldn't face the long walk barefoot. I let my hat float on the water. If they thought me drowned, so much the better. At the last moment I remembered Duncan, and went back. He was still stunned. I bent down and made sure he was not shamming, then loosened the cords at his feet and freed his hands completely. I wondered what tale he would tell his confederates.

The water was icy cold, for the storm had stirred up the depths. But at least it shocked me into full wakefulness, and ended that half-dazed condition I had been in since my fall. I knew I had got a fight on. This was no sunny bathing trip. I lacked sleep. I had had little food, and I was still suffering from a tremendous crack on the head. Half-way across, I began to doubt if I should ever manage it.

I set my teeth and ploughed on towards that green line of woods. The shoes tugged at the waist of my pants. It was like dragging an iron fetter. The water slapped me in the face and my limbs ached . . .

I mustn't give up. I mustn't give up. I think I panted the words aloud, above the roaring in my ears. Everything depended on my reaching that thin line of grey shingle, that fringe of oaks and pines. If I gave up now, and let myself slip down into the sweet peace of green water, the Queen would be murdered and the kingdom thrown into anarchy. Thousands of Englishmen would die in the quarrel. English homes would flare skywards, English women and children would run shrieking to the safety of forest and fell, and the horror our people had not known for years would come again.

That was what kept me swimming. It wasn't just the life of an old lady with a crown. It was for all of us. No one in England knew what I knew – except the conspirators whose mad dreams were rushing us towards this horror. I mustn't sink, with that secret, into the lake.

The trees, which seemed to have stood still for so long, leapt suddenly nearer. As I rose on the swell I could peer into the wood and see the road looping down over a hump in the bank. I caught glimpses of outcrop rock clothed in lichen. Once I saw a rabbit bolt into a clump of fern. I put my foot down, hardly daring to hope, and touched bottom.

Safe! I staggered up the shelving beach, my under-clothes skin-tight, and dropped down sobbing with exhaustion. In a few minutes I felt better, and was able to cram my cold feet into my sodden shoes. I had still before me a tramp of seven miles or more to Lonsdale, but I could face that almost cheerfully. I wasn't sure, within a mile or so, of my exact whereabouts, but I guessed that if I found a valley leading off at right angles to the lake, and followed it up, bearing north-westwards across the fells, I should be able to reach home soon after dusk.

Once more, however, my plans were destined to be upset. I hadn't walked a hundred yards down the road before I heard voices. Half a dozen horses were crop-ping the grass, and as many men were walking down to a boat which had been drawn up on the shingle.

I turned back hurriedly, but my white figure must have been noticed racing through the trees, and I heard shouts behind me. At first I ran blindly forward along the road, past where I had landed, and on up the valley towards Patterdale, but I soon realized, from the drum-ming of hooves, that my pursuers had remounted and that it was sheer suicide to keep to a road which horses could follow.

A track turned off to the right, away from the lake, and I took it. Quite a broad valley opened before me, with a good-sized beck, storm-swollen, boiling down the middle of it, and the valley-head closed by a great mountain – Raise, I suppose, or one of the other peaks in the Helvellyn range. I saw it for only a moment, black and swart against the westering sun, and it promised safety. Then a cloud rolled over the summit and my hope was hidden.

I must leave the track at once. I dropped down the long bank, splashed through the beck, and set myself to the slope beyond. A pistol cracked – I must have made a fine target – but the range was too great. I was glad none of my pursuers had a long-bow. That would have been a different thing.

Sir Philip's voice reached me, if his bullet didn't.

'Not *all* of you! He may double back to the road!'

It wasn't long before my bursting heart made me pause on the roof-like hillside, and there was no harm then in glancing back. Only two men had left their horses to clamber after me. The others were riding away.

I saw the game. There was only the one road, running north and south along the lakeside. North to Penrith, south over the Kirkstone Pass to Kendal and . . . London. It was the easiest thing in the world to cut that lifeline at a couple of places, and leave me no escape save by crossing the wall of mountains in front of me.

Well, I was prepared to. I wanted to get home and rejoin Kit, anyhow. I had no intention of doubling back to the road. It would be a race between me and the two men behind. If I'd been fresh, I'd have snapped my fingers at them. As it was, I felt less happy about the result.

There was no cover on these slopes; the woods were far below. There was mist above. If I could reach that with sufficient lead over the men, and if the mist proved thick enough, I might manage to give them the slip.

These fells were strange to me and I had to go by guesswork. There was a steep slope in front, and I toiled up it. Up . . . all the time, up . . . Nothing else much mattered.

Behind me clambered my two pursuers, grim as bloodhounds on a scent. A man in green and black led, by half a dozen yards, a heavier fellow in a scarlet doublet. The first man scarcely showed against the tough moor-grass; I only saw him plainly when he topped some crest and was outlined for a moment against the pale sky of evening. His companion I could see vividly whenever I turned my head. He stood out like a blood-splash on the shoulder of the land.

They never shouted to me, knowing that it would be useless and they might as well save their breath. They came on patiently, with a quiet confidence that was more terrifying than any bellowed threats. They were so sure it was just a matter of time before they caught up with me.

We weren't running. There was no more run left in us for the time being. If you'd come upon us that evening, three strung-out figures plodding up and up, you would never have thought that this deliberate clamber was a race for life. Well, if any of us could have moved faster, you may be assured that we should.

We were very high now. The world below us slanted and reeled away into dizzy valleys, already purple with the brimming dusk. The upper reaches of Ullswater lay like a jagged piece of glass. The water was tufted with tree-clad islets, looking small as bees.

Up here it was still broad daylight, with a bronze glimmer of sun behind the drifting cloud-wrack. The clouds were not so far ahead now.

I judged that I had missed the easy passes which cross this range, and must be climbing one of the main peaks, possibly Helvellyn itself. It behoved me to go warily, or as warily as those human hounds would let me. There were ugly precipices in these parts. I wasn't afraid of them, but I was afraid of landing myself in some dead end, with no choice but to drop or be caught. This mist might prove an enemy no less than a friend.

I know now where we were that evening. I've even grown to love the grim place. But then, when I saw it for the first time with the men at my heels, it was only terrifying.

For a mile or more I had been coming up a long grassy ridge, with the slope gradual enough for me to run a little way from time to time. Now I topped the ridge and found myself at the left-hand tip of a mighty horseshoe of precipices.

In front ran the knife-back of Striding Edge, with a sickening drop for hundreds of feet on either side. A knife-back did I say? No, a saw rather, for it was all jagged with rocks.

Over to my right, across a great emptiness of air, was the other side of the horseshoe, Swirral Edge, showing a precipice no less ugly. Joining the two Edges together, and forming the bend of the horse-shoe, was a towering mass higher than either. Even at the time I knew this must be Helvellyn, though its shape was largely obscured by racing tatters of cloud.

I glanced back. The man in green had fallen back a little, but his friend was overhauling me rapidly, as though he had begun to draw on some reserve of strength.

I set my face to the craggy spine before me, and forced my aching legs to carry me on.

It was windy up here. Hot as I was, I felt it strike chilly against my half-clad body. The rocks were greasy with a fine rain. The clouds swirled about me, taking the colour out of the landscape and reducing everything to a vague grey, but there was no mist dense enough to hide me from my enemies.

I scrambled along, hoisting myself over the rocks, squeezing between them, swinging round them with desperate fingers, and nothing to save me if I let go. On my left hand the world fell away into what looked, from the glimpses I caught through shreds of cloud, to be a bottomless abyss. It is well named Nethermost Cove. On my right – and for the most part I tried to keep to this side of the Edge – I could see down into the centre of the horseshoe. There was a big tarn down there, walled in by the curving precipices like the tarn at the Stronghold, but four times as big. At some moments I could see it plainly beneath me, inky black; then it would mist over like a mirror, and I could see only a pale glimmer of silver through the intervening clouds, or nothing at all.

My breath came in sobs. My legs were leaden. The

blood welled from a dozen smarting grazes. I struggled on, but I knew the end was near.

There was one place where I had to mount a flat rock and take a few paces along the very crest of the ridge, with no support on either side. The wind rocked me as I stood upright, and for a moment I thought I was lost. I dropped to my knees and crawled across.

I glanced back when I'd scrambled another twenty yards. The man in the scarlet doublet was already coming over the high rock. His feet were planted well apart, he bent confidently against the tugging wind, his arms were stretched to balance . . . and soon to clutch . . .

If only I had my pistol I could have dropped him like a rabbit. But he knew I was unarmed. He came on with a triumphant smile curving his lips.

We were nearly across the Edge. At the other end it dips a little; you have to squeeze yourself down a crack in the rock. Then there's a narrow saddle curving down and up, a sort of isthmus linking the Edge with the main mass of the mountain. No more crags – just sliding scree, millions of tiny loose stones, and a tuft of coarse grass here and there.

But that evening I didn't find the crack at first. I went wrong by a yard or two, and worked myself out on to a promontory from which there was no way forward. The cold air walled me in.

I backed hurriedly. I saw the nick in the rocks now, and began to lower myself down, scraping and bruising my hips considerably. But the delay cost me dear.

The foremost of my pursuers was upon me.

'You little fox!' he panted, baring his teeth under his black moustache. 'A fine chase you've given us!'

I knew it was useless to run on, but I wouldn't give in tamely. I was in a good position, feet firm and braced. He, for his part, was over-confident, seeing only an exhausted youth, slim for his age.

We faced each other, two tiny creatures on a soaring pinnacle of crag. That crag, at that moment was our whole world. A cloud had swept over the saddle. Red Tarn was gone, Nethermost Cove was gone. The whiteness had washed over everything. Seeing us, you would have thought we stood on cloud.

The scarlet doublet loomed above me. The fawn hose dangled as the feet groped for hold. I saw my chance. It was easy enough for anyone who had ever wrestled and had any idea of what can be done by applying all one's strength at a single decisive point.

I jumped for one of those legs and twisted it sideways. The man swore, then cried out in panic. He lashed out with his free leg, and it was lucky that none of his

kicks landed, or I should have been pushed over the edge.

I increased the pressure. I don't like remembering this, but it was his life or mine. I peeled him from his hold on the rock-face, and he crashed down ten feet, head-first into the scree. I'd hoped he would lie there, stunned and perhaps injured enough to make his companion give up the chase. But he bounced sideways and went rolling down into the mist-brimmed gulf of Nethermost Cove. He was lost to sight almost immediately, but for ages, as it seemed, I could hear the trickle of scree, like shingle on the beach, following him as he rolled over and over.

I went shakily across the saddle and bent myself to the last gruelling ascent of the peak. When I forced myself to look back, I saw the second man crouching where we had struggled, peering down into the clouds.

I climbed on, and he did not follow me.

19.

Besieged

The dog burst into a fury of barking as I staggered up to the door of our farm, and it's no wonder he didn't recognize that white bedraggled spectre as one of the family.

'Down, Snap!' I tried to say, but the words were soundless on my lips.

The door opened, and there stood Kit against the candlelight. She screamed as I staggered forward, and I thought she was frightened, not knowing me, but it was horror at my graveyard look. She put her arms under mine and guided me across the doorstep. I heard her say, 'It's Peter!' and my mother exclaim, 'Thank God!'

'They've beaten him!' said Kit, and it was the only time I have heard her cry.

'No,' I said huskily, collapsing on the settee. 'I – I've had a long walk – and a swim – and before that I fell down. That's all.' And suddenly I realized how funny it all sounded, and I began to laugh hysterically.

The next thing I knew I was warm and dry in bed, and they were kneeling one on either side, plying me with food.

'He'll be all right after a good sleep,' said Mother cheerfully. She was used to her menfolk coming home half-dead, especially in winter, and it took a lot to send her into a panic.

I couldn't sleep, though, till I had asked one or two questions.

They told me that all the neighbours were armed and out, searching Blencathra and the surrounding fells for me or my body. As soon as Kit had brought the news, Dad had mustered the neighbours and they'd marched to the peel-tower. There'd been no one there, so they'd battered down the door and ransacked the place from roof to cellar. They'd found nothing. 'No,' said Kit, catching my look and my thought, 'not even –' She didn't finish, but I knew she meant, as I meant, poor Tom Boyd. Evidently the conspirators, scared by the discovery of another spy so soon after the first, had abandoned their headquarters at a moment's notice, making a clean sweep of any evidence which might have served to incriminate them.

'Everything's all right; don't worry,' said Mother,

patting my pillow. 'Tom and your dad will be in soon; they've got the business in hand, and those scoundrels won't get within a mile of you again.'

I grinned weakly. This was going back to childhood with a vengeance, back to the comforting little world in which Father and Big Brother can save one from every possible peril.

I couldn't go back like that. These last months had made a man of me, perhaps a little before my time, and, man-like, I had to stand on my own feet.

'Dad can't save the Queen's life in London,' I said. 'Now Tom Boyd . . . hasn't come back, I've got to take on his work.'

'And I,' whispered Kit.

Then I poured out the story of what I'd heard in the peel-tower – the plot to assassinate the Queen, to set the North of England aflame with rebellion, and to call in a Spanish fleet. I *had* to share the secret quickly. It was too big a burden to carry alone. I might be ill in the morning; I might have a raging fever and be out of the fight for days. But Kit, I knew, would send the news if I couldn't.

'First thing in the morning,' I said hoarsely, 'we find someone we can trust – a magistrate – and have word sent to London. That's *got* to be done. Understand?'

'Of course,' Kit said.

'And now sleep,' said Mother decidedly, taking the empty soup-bowl from my fingers and tucking the bed-clothes round my shoulders. 'Good night, Pete,' Kit murmured, and they put out the light. They went away into the kitchen, the door closed softly behind them, and that, for me, was the end of a very strenuous day.

When I opened my eyes, Kit was bending over me. 'I thought you were never going to wake again! Ready for food?'

'Rather!'

'Your mother's on to me to wear some of your sister's clothes,' she said, with a grin, as she sauntered away to the kitchen, 'but I'm staying a man till this thing's finished. He's awake,' she called as she passed through the doorway.

The family gathered round while I sat up and ate. All except my brother, that is: he was out at work, for the daily round of a farm must somehow go on. My father was in his best clothes, and he sat on a stool with his broad hands laid on his knees. He said:

'Well, young man, this has been a grand to-do! Soon as you're up and dressed, we're going to ride straight into Keswick to see Mr Armthwaite. We'll tell him the whole story. He's a Justice of the Peace. He'll know what to do.'

I looked at Dad, and I thought to myself he was taking charge a bit too readily. Wasn't I a Secret Agent of Her Majesty? Then I looked at Dad again, and decided it wouldn't be at all wise to argue with him. I might rise to the dizziest heights and become Baron Brownrigg of Lonsdale and be the Queen's Principal Secretary of State, but to Dad I'd never be anything but his son.

Anyhow, what he said fitted in perfectly with my own plans. Mr Armthwaite, living in his big mansion in Keswick, was as handy a magistrate as we could choose, and he would be able to set the machinery of the law in motion at once. The main thing was to have the warning message dispatched to Sir Robert in London, ensuring the arrest of Somers and all necessary precautions at the performance. I only hoped, for the sake of Shakespeare and all our friends, that they wouldn't call off the play entirely. It wouldn't be like Elizabeth to agree to that.

The performance was now six days distant. I wasn't sure how fast the Government couriers could travel, but I guessed that, with fresh horses ready at every stage and summer weather to favour them, the news should reach Sir Robert within two or three days. That would allow plenty of time for counter-measures in London. The northern ringleaders would presumably be under arrest, and the rising stifled before London was even aware of the danger.

I got out of bed and put on clean shoes. They were clothes I hadn't worn since I left home, and I got a shock to find how short in the sleeve and tight across the shoulders they were. Apart from a few tender places where I had scratched or bruised myself, I felt none the worse for my adventures. I'd been living roughly for so long.

Just as I passed through into the kitchen and said I was ready, my brother Tom came striding in, the axe dangling in his hand.

'Sir Philip's coming up our way,' he said quietly.

Dad looked at him. 'Alone?'

'Not likely! There's five of 'em.'

'Give me that axe, lad. I'll finish splitting those logs for you.' Outside, the dog gave loud warning that strangers were getting near. 'Kit and Peter must hide upstairs in the loft. The rest of you carry on with your ordinary jobs. And mind, now – you none of you know anything, beyond what I say.'

'Do be careful,' begged my mother as he went out.

'I'll be careful of myself,' he promised, smiling back over his shoulder from the door.

I took Kit's hand. 'Come on; we'd better do as Dad says.' There was a small loft over the bedroom upstairs, and we made ourselves comfortable along the beams. A few chinks of sunlight showed between the roof-slabs, and we could hear the voices outside quite plainly.

'Good morning, Mr Brownrigg,' said Sir Philip very civilly.

'Morning, Sir Philip. What can I do for you?'

'I want to know where your younger son is.'

'So do I,' said Dad shortly.

'You surely don't mean that *you* don't know?'

'Well,' rumbled my father, 'seeing that I was out looking for him on the fells all yesterday till long after dark, with most of the neighbours helping . . . 'Tisn't likely we'd do that if we knew where he was. Is it? I may be a fool, but my neighbours aren't.'

'Yesterday isn't today.'

'No, but today'll soon be yesterday if we stand wasting time like this.' And I heard the ring of the axe as Dad brought it down on a log, splitting it cleanly. I should think Sir Philip felt glad the blow hadn't landed on his own head.

Kit nudged me in the darkness. 'I like your father,' she whispered.

'There's no need to waste any of your time,' said Sir Philip coldly. 'I just want to look inside your house, and I can do that without your assistance.'

'You can do nothing of the sort, Sir Philip. My house

is my house. And no one enters without my invitation. There's not many men in Cumberland who wouldn't be right welcome, but I'm sorry to say you're one of the few.'

'Indeed? If you are going to take that line, I can produce a warrant signed by magistrates –'

'No doubt! Friends of yours!'

'You don't seem to realize the position, Brownrigg. Your son is a dangerous young criminal.'

'I know – you say he slung a stone at you last year!'

'It may be news to you that within the last twenty-four hours he has savagely assaulted two other gentlemen. Sir Walter Percy may not recover.' (He must be tough, I thought to myself, to have survived that roll down the scree at all.)

'Ay,' said my father meaningly, 'there's been a deal of lawbreaking in these parts lately. I only hope everyone comes to the justice he deserves.'

'Including your son?'

'Everyone guilty. No matter who it is.' At that I can imagine he gave Sir Philip a straight look which the knight didn't relish. Then Dad's voice changed. It was sharp now. 'If those friends of yours go any nearer my door, I won't answer for what happens to them!'

'Come on!' Sir Philip shouted. 'It's quite clear he's got the young scoundrel inside!'

There was a confused din then a frantic dog and rearing horses. A pistol snapped and the bullet thudded against the house.

'Come on,' I said, and dropped down from the loft. At the same moment the door slammed downstairs with an echoing crash, and by the time we reached the kitchen it was safely barred. I was relieved to see Dad unhurt.

'Best barricade the windows,' he ordered. Luckily, they were small, and it was an easy matter to block them. All the time we were doing it, Sir Philip's friends were kicking and hammering at the door.

'They'll not break that down in a hurry,' said my brother. 'What else shall we do, Dad? I wish we'd a musket.'

'The old long-bow's a sight better than any musket,' said my father, who was conservative in many ways and could never see that gunpowder had been a useful addition to life.

'But it makes no noise,' Tom explained. 'If we'd a musket and fired it off, maybe the Bells or some of the other neighbours would hear it and come along.'

'I've a pistol,' said Kit, pulling out the one Tom Boyd had given her.

'So have we – and one of those fellows outside has already fired his. But they only make a bit of a snap: they'd not be heard down the dale.'

'Bide quiet a minute,' said Dad. 'They've stopped beating on the door. What are they up to?'

We all listened. Our besiegers had moved away. We could hear only a distant murmur of voices in consultation. We couldn't make out what they were saying.

'I suppose they couldn't break in anyhow at the back?' Kit asked.

'No; there's only that tiny slit of a window to keep the dairy cool. They'd never get through that,' said Mother.

It was lucky that our house backed so closely on the mountainside, so that there were no doors or windows to guard there.

'I'm going upstairs to see what they're doing,' I said, and ran up to the little bedroom window, low under the eaves, which gave a clear view of all that was going on in front of the house.

All the men had dismounted, and their horses were grazing beside the beck. The men – among whom I recognized our old adversary, the yellow gentleman, though now very foppishly dressed in pale lilac – were grouped round a log which was lying ready to be turned into fuel. I saw their idea at once.

'They're going to use that log as a battering-ram!' I called down to the family.

'Let them try,' growled my father. He came tramping slowly upstairs, and I saw that the old bow was ready strung in his hand. 'Hold those arrows,' he ordered. 'I may need them in a hurry.'

We waited tensely. Outside, it was just an ordinary summer's day. The beck sang the same rippling song which had been part of my life ever since I could remember. The hens strutted hither and thither, scratching for food, sublimely indifferent to the human combat. Only Snap skirmished round, snarling at the intruders.

The men picked up the length of tree-trunk, two each side, for it was not long enough to provide hand-hold for six. Neither Sir Philip nor Sir David helped, but they drew their rapiers, as if to lead the assault once a breach was made.

'That's a good weight of timber,' grunted Dad, without taking his eyes off them. 'But I didn't fell it for this. Give me an arrow.'

He drew back the bow-string and let fly. There was a yelp of pain from the group, and I saw that one man's hand was pinned to the log. His friends helped to draw out the arrow, and he danced away, swearing and clutching his wound. The log was dropped hurriedly, and they all withdrew behind some trees. It looked as if the battering-ram idea was unpopular.

'The next one,' Dad announced calmly, 'will be a leg or a shoulder.' He might have been discussing joints for dinner, he was so quiet about it. 'But if I have to shoot a third time, it's Sir Philip, heart or throat. And hang the consequences! A man must defend his own home and his folk.'

Sir Philip had no intention, apparently, of exposing himself to such peril. I caught a glimpse of him in the deep shade of the sycamores, pointing and gesticulating. Suddenly two of the men dashed forward, grabbed the log, and hauled it away into cover. My father kept his arrow notched on the string. He would not shoot unless they approached the house.

'I see their game,' I said. 'They're going to sneak round the side, behind the stone fence.'

'Let them. They can't batter down solid walls.'

'No, Dad, but they can get to the door that way without coming straight at us across the open ground.'

'You're right, Peter.' Dad knitted his brow, stooped down and peered through the little window. Our walls were so thick that we couldn't see the ground immediately in front of the house. There was a strip ten paces deep which was hidden from us – ample space for the men to swing their ram, if they could get there without crossing the danger zone. They could do it, too, by creeping up to the house from the flank.

'We can drop boiling water on their heads,' he said cheerfully, and shouted down to Mother to see that the biggest pot should be ready on the hearth.

'We can't hold them off for ever like that, Dad,' said my brother, joining us at the window. 'We'll have to get help somehow.'

'How?'

'If you threw open the door suddenly and I ran out, and then you barred it quick behind me, I reckon I could take them by surprise. I'd get down to Bell's and rouse up the whole dale. We'd chase these chaps off in no time.'

'It's too risky, lad.'

Tom looked hurt. 'It's time I took a few risks,' he grumbled.

'I've a better idea,' I said. 'Suppose I squeezed through the little dairy window? The fern's standing tall at the back of the house. I could creep right along to the waterfall, and then down the new fence; there's a good cover half-way to Bell's.'

'Not even you could get through that window,' said Dad.

'I could – at least, I could once.' I flushed at the memory. One day when I'd been in disgrace, and forbidden to leave the house, I'd sneaked out by that very way and in again two hours afterwards. My father had been working in front of the house the whole time, and he'd never seen me crawling through the bracken on the mountainside above. Yes, I knew what I was talking about. But that had been two or three years ago, and I was smaller then.

'If Pete's too fat, I might manage it,' said Kit.

At another time we might have argued for some time as to which of the two was the rounder at the part most likely to stick in a window-frame, but the situation was too serious. We ran downstairs and into the dim room at the back, where the air always struck as cold as a cave. I pushed aside a pan of milk and knelt on the stone slab. The window was tall but very thin, and the great thickness of our walls did not help matters. Still, by wriggling and scraping my shoulders, and letting Kit shove vigorously from the rear, I succeeded at last in popping out of that hole like a bung out of a barrel.

Kit followed. I got hold of her under the armpits and pulled, and she knocked me backwards into the bracken as she came.

'You'd best not come back yourselves,' said Dad, putting his head through.

'Not come back?'

'No, till we know how this little to-do is going to end. Just tell the neighbours, and they'll see we're all right. Once you're out of the way, you'd better keep out of the way. Those horses you brought are still waiting in Mr Bell's stable. You'd best make for Keswick at once, while Sir Philip's occupied here, and see Mr Armthwaite.'

'All right, Dad. Good-bye!' We dropped on all fours and slid through that bracken like adders.

20.

Then Who is Loyal?

We crossed the beck just above the waterfall, and then there was still better cover, for a stone wall, which we always called 'the new fence', though it had been built by my grandfather, ran most of the way along the fellside to the next farm. We were able to stand up here and peep.

The besiegers were moving stealthily into position, making a wide circle round the flank of the house so that Dad couldn't get them within bowshot. Even with the help of Mother's cauldron of boiling water, I didn't think the door could be held more than ten or fifteen minutes. After that, I think Dad's plan was to retreat upstairs, behind a barricade of furniture, and try to keep the men at bay till help arrived. I hoped matters would not reach that pass. I was afraid Sir Philip might set the house on fire.

Luckily, the wall was a high one and we no longer had to crawl. We ran at full pelt, and I'm bound to say that when I rushed panting into Bell's farmyard, Kit wasn't ten yards behind.

We gasped out our story and, without more ado, began to saddle the horses we had ridden from London. Mr Bell called to his sons and fetched his pike from the kitchen.

'We'll go straight up along,' he said quietly. 'If you see any of the other neighbours as you go down the road, tell 'em to follow on.'

'I will,' I said.

Our Cumbrian statesmen are the best neighbours in the world. Lose yourself in the snow or twist your ankle on the crags, they'll turn out uncomplainingly to help. During this last year our people in Lonsdale had got particularly neighbourly, for they knew they had an enemy in common. The theft of their common lands had first rallied them against Sir Philip and the events of the last day or two (though they had only a faint glimmering notion of what it was all about) had knit them into a closer comradeship. Sir Philip might be within his strict legal rights in bringing a warrant to search our house, but we statesmen had learnt that legal rights were not everything. They knew Dad was their friend and Sir Philip their enemy. Though they swung for it in Carlisle market-place, they were not going to stand by while a Brownrigg was in trouble.

So, as we galloped down the dale, our shouts brought the menfolk of every family running together, and in twos and threes, armed with every kind of weapon from a pitchfork to a crossbow, they went hurrying up the road to strike a blow at their local tyrant.

'I feel ashamed to be leaving this,' I said as we turned on to the main road.

'They have plenty without us, Pete. We've something still more important.'

'And we'd better hurry,' I said, with a laugh, 'or Sir Philip's crew will come pelting out of the dale in such a panic that we'll find them on our heels.' I wasn't seriously afraid of that, because Sir Philip was much more likely to run for the safety of his big new house, and that lay in the opposite direction, Penrith way.

Our horses were poorish beasts, for it would not have done for pedlar's boys to be too well mounted, but they were quite fresh and skittish after two or three days' rest in the stable. As it was mostly downhill to Keswick, we clattered along at a good speed.

'Thank goodness this is nearly over,' said Kit. 'Excitement's all very well, but this has been a bit too much.'

I agreed that I shouldn't be sorry when we had handed over our responsibilities to Mr Armthwaite. With our dispatch on its way to Sir Robert, with the forces of law and order mustering throughout the North, and with our own special enemy under lock and key, we should be able to feel that we could take life easily again.

'Plenty to eat,' I said.

'And plenty of sleep.'

'And a nice long swim in Derwentwater.'

She burst out laughing at that. 'Wasn't Ullswater yesterday enough for you?'

'I don't want to see Ullswater again for a long time.'

'It's the loveliest lake in the world,' she snorted. 'Don't forget I've got a house beside it, and some day I'm going to live there again.'

That friendly argument kept us going as far as the town. The gentleman we were seeking lived on the far side of Keswick, close to Crosthwaite, and we passed several people I knew as we rode through the narrow streets. Some waved and shouted to me, others just stared with fallen jaws, as if I were a ghost, but I stopped for nobody. It would be pleasant to meet old friends when this matter was settled and I could walk the roads again without fear of interference. Just now I was too occupied with the work in hand.

'What if he's not at home?' asked Kit.

'Plenty of other magistrates. But we won't turn back: we'll ride straight on till we do find someone.'

But we were fortunate. We caught Mr Armthwaite just as he was leaving. A groom was walking two horses up and down in front of the steps – lovely glossy creatures, a roan gelding and a black mare. Mr Armthwaite had the reputation of being a fine judge of horseflesh.

He came down the steps as we dismounted, a brisk little grey man, with a beard which looked as though it were frosted over, and questing eyes. I knew him by sight, but I don't suppose he knew me from Adam.

'You want to see me, my lad? I'm in rather a hurry.'

'It's important, sir.'

'Oh; then, what is it?'

I glanced at the groom. I didn't want to take any chances. 'If you don't mind, sir, it's rather confidential. Perhaps – might we go indoors?'

He gave me a quick, sharp look and an understanding smile. 'Very well, my lad, perhaps you're wise. Come along in, come along in.' He beckoned us up the steps, and led the way across a spacious hall, upstairs, and along a gallery. 'In here, boys.' We followed him into a panelled room with rows and rows of books and a magnificent window with coats of arms in coloured glass. I glanced through and saw a rose-garden underneath and a peacock marching up and down like a sentinel. Mr Armthwaite lived in great style.

Once the door was closed behind us, he became even brisker, if possible, than before.

'Out with it, lad. No one can hear us here.' He fussed across to the window and shut the casement portion, which had been open.

I told him, with a little prompting and correction from Kit, the story of our investigations and the discoveries we had made. He sat in his armchair with his finger-tips pressed together, saying nothing but 'Dear me!' at intervals. When I had finished, he said:

'And what do you wish me to do?'

I looked a little surprised at that. 'Well,' I said, 'I suppose you will do what seems best to you.'

'Certainly, certainly.' He smiled encouragingly. 'I shall inform the necessary authorities. Dear me, it *is* lucky you came to me, my lad, and found me in! You might have gone to some of our magistrates with this story, and the result might have been quite disastrous. They might have told *entirely* the wrong people, and that would never have done.'

I was a little puzzled by this tone, but I supposed it was his quaint elderly way. Men like magistrates sometimes behave oddly, I've noticed, because they are such important people that no one they know dares to criticize them to their faces.

'Yes,' he said, with a dry little chuckle, and he strutted

across the polished floor to where an orange bell-cord dangled against the panelling. 'It would never have done for this news to fall into the wrong hands. All our plans would have been quite upset. I can't tell you how vexed we should have been if –'

'If you touch that bell-cord,' said Kit in a high, nervous voice behind me, 'you'll get something that will upset you still more!'

Mr Armthwaite turned, his jaw dropping, and I too spun round with a gasp of shocked amazement. Kit was standing very pale and tight-lipped, waggling her pistol in the direction of the magistrate.

'What's up, you idiot?' I demanded.

'What is the meaning of –' Mr Armthwaite began, but she cut him short rudely. I don't suppose he'd been interrupted so sharply in all the years he had sat on the Bench.

'*You* know,' she said. 'Stand away from that bell. That's better. Keep quite still. Pete, lock the door and put the key in your pocket. Don't stand gaping! This man's as bad as the rest of them. Why were you going to ring the bell?' she snapped at him, jabbing the air with her pistol.

'My dear lad,' said Mr Armthwaite, recovering his poise a little, 'have you taken leave of your senses? There's nothing in ringing a bell. There are letters to be written and sent –'

'But not the letters *we* want written, or sent to the right people. It's Sir Philip Morton you mean to warn – and goodness knows what you'd do with us, to keep us quiet.' She spoke to me then, without taking her eyes off the old gentleman. 'We've been unlucky, Pete. We've picked on another of that crew. We'd better get out of here.'

'Give me the pistol,' I said, and we made the exchange neatly, without for a second leaving Mr Armthwaite uncovered. His foxy eyes were questing round the room, and the truth of what Kit had said was written in his face.

'What about the window?' I suggested.

Kit went to it and opened the casement. The fragrance of early roses and wet earth came flooding back into the room.

'You and I could drop down here,' she said, 'but I don't think Mr Armthwaite's old bones would be improved by it!'

'Good! Out you go, Kit, and run round to where we left the horses. I'll give you a minute's start, then I'll follow.'

She swung her leg over the sill obediently. From the corner of my eye I saw her grubby brown hands cling for a moment, then let go. There was a dull thud from below.

'You young rascals!' Mr Armthwaite broke out. 'My roses!'

Funny how a man who had suddenly seen himself brought within the shadow of the scaffold displayed more concern for his precious flowers than for his own neck!

'Stand right over there,' I told him. I backed to the window, keeping him covered till the last possible moment. Then I turned and took a flying leap, landing on all fours in the soft earth and manure of the rose-bed. I picked myself up in a trice, and raced round the corner of the house. Somewhere within I heard a bell jangling as if the ringer had gone crazy.

Kit was already mounted. The groom was still patiently walking the roan and the black up and down.

In for a penny, in for a pound, I said to myself. There, in front of us, was the best horseflesh in the neighbourhood, ready saddled and all. If we took it, we could show a clean set of heels to any pursuer. If we left it to our enemies we should be overtaken on our poor hacks before we had ridden a mile.

'We're changing horses,' I gasped to Kit, and I stuck the pistol under the groom's red nose. 'Stand back! Let go those bridles, or –'

He could see I meant it. He dropped back a few paces, gibbering with indignation and amazement. Kit needed no prompting; you could always rely on her to play up, and she was already astride the black mare.

'*I've* a bullet for you, too, if you try any tricks!' she called blood-thirstily; and by the time his eyes had swung round to her (as she knew they would) and he'd realized that she was actually unarmed, the ruse had served its purpose by giving me time to mount. The gelding danced skittishly as I dropped into the saddle, and I felt the joy that every man must feel when his knees first grip so superb an animal.

Just then the most frightful hullabaloo of women arose inside the house, and a servant-girl appeared screeching at the top of the steps.

'Come quick, Joe! The master's locked in! He wants the ladder 'gainst the window!'

It was high time to be gone. I pressed the sides of the roan gelding, and he sprang forward with a scattering of gravel. Kit galloped half a length behind, and our old hacks, puzzled by this new arrangement, came racing behind us with streaming tails and manes, as if determined not to miss the fun.

Through the gates we swept, and along the road, with the shouts and screams fading behind us. At the first corner we almost rode down my old schoolmaster, who was stumping along with his head down and his favourite volume of Horace tucked under his arm.

'Brownrigg!' he thundered as he raised his eyes and recognized me. 'Stop, boy! Dismount from that –'

But the rest of his words were choked by the fine June dust we had stirred as we swept by. Glancing back, I saw a dim figure brandishing that stick which I knew all too well. It was hard to realize that, to him, Peter Brownrigg was just one of the bigger boys who'd left school rather suddenly and disgracefully a year before. He'd never heard of Peter Brownrigg the actor or Peter Brownrigg the Secret Agent! Why don't old people realize how quickly a boy grows up?

'Which way?' panted Kit.

Her eyes were shining. She rode the mare as though the pair of them were one creature – a centaur.

'Through the town, then south.' It was no good turning home again. We might run our heads straight into more trouble.

We slowed to a trot as we passed through Keswick. There was no sense in attracting too much attention by dangerous riding in the narrow streets, though we couldn't expect to escape notice entirely. Mr Armthwaite's horses were of the kind that make men's heads turn appreciatively, and to see them ridden by boys was at least unusual.

'We seem to have left our old friends behind,' I said, meaning the horses. They had soon tired of the gallop.

'Fair exchange,' said Kit. 'But I don't see Mr Armthwaite and his man catching us on *those* mounts.'

'How on earth did you guess he was in the plot?' I asked as we set our faces to the long climb up the shoulder of Castlerigg Fell.

'Because he pretended he didn't know Sir Philip personally when you started your story. He was nervous then. He didn't know how things were going to turn out, and he was playing for safety. If he'd found it was all up with the plot, he'd have gone on denying that he knew Philip. But he does. I remember his face. They've dined at my guardian's on the same day, and I've watched them talking.'

'It was lucky you did what you did,' I said thankfully. 'I can see his game now, of course. He'd have called his servants –'

'And good-bye to all hope of sending that message to London!'

'Phew! What a narrow escape!'

We rode on in silence for a little way. Keswick lay beneath us in the green bowl of its valley, encircled by Skiddaw and the other fells. As yet there was no speck of pursuit on the winding road we had traversed.

'It's wicked!' she burst out. 'The whole countryside is riddled with treason – even the magistrates. Who *is* loyal? Who *can* be trusted?'

I shrugged my shoulders. I could answer for most of the ordinary folk, like the statesmen of our own dale, but they couldn't send the urgent code message to the Government for which the situation called. The men who could have helped – magistrates, sheriffs, noblemen . . . Was there one I could name, and feel positive he wouldn't serve us as Mr Armthwaite had tried to do? So many of these families had taken part in the Rising of the North when Dad was a boy. Memories linger long in the dales, and there must be many who were ready to seek revenge.

'Can you think of anyone?' Kit insisted.

'No, I can't.'

'Then, what do you propose?'

I bent forward and patted the horse's satin neck. 'We must depend on ourselves alone – and these beauties. There's plenty of time, and we shan't be caught easily. We'd better ride to London and tell Sir Robert the news ourselves.'

'I'm ready to, if you are,' she said.

'Good!'

I twisted in my saddle and looked back down the hill. Was it fancy, or was there already a dust-cloud rolling along upon our trail?

21.

The Road Lay Open

T he road lay open before us, ribboning on by mountain and valley, heath and forest, for three hundred
miles. We had nothing to do but ride. After the past
few days, so packed with mysteries and misadventures,
it was a relief to find ourselves with so simple and
straightforward a task.

Our horses made light of the stiff climb from
Keswick, for we were only featherweights to carry.
Soon the road levelled out and we were able to set
them to a trot again. We came round the steep wooded
knoll of Great Howe, and there was the long streak of
Thirlmere, lying in its crack between Helvellyn and the
Armboth fells.

'Come on!' cried Kit, and set the mare to a canter. I
dug in my heels and shot level with her, and we thundered along the lakeside road, knee to knee.

Rub-a-dub, rub-a-dub, rub-a-dub . . .

Is there any drum which beats a more stirring tattoo than hooves on the hard-trampled earth?

Rub-a-dub, rub-a-dub, rub-a-dub . . .

Past the ancient bridge which spans the shallows and narrows of the mere, and links the two mansions of Dalehead and Armboth Hall . . . Were they in the conspiracy, I wondered, the Jacksons over the bridge and the Leathes at Dalehead, nestling between the lake and the road? I hoped not, for they were good old statesmen families, both of them, but we weren't going to take chances by turning aside to ask their help. We rode on . . .

Helvellyn Gill came splashing across our road. Helvellyn Screes came sweeping down, the stony slopes looking in the heat-mist of noon as light and insubstantial as a grey silk hanging. Our road was the fringe or the hem, and the feathery trees were like tassels along the water's edge beneath us.

Rub-a-dub, rub-a-dub . . .

Into the scorching sunshine, then into green shade again, cool as a spring . . .

Looking across the mere, we watched the landmarks creep behind us: Raven Crag, Fisher Crag, Launchy Gill – its cascades spilling down the green fellside like milk – Hause Point, Dob Gill.

We didn't talk much for a time. We were too excited by the rhythm of the hoof-music and the wine-like air rushing into our nostrils and between our parted lips.

There would soon, I thought, be a very different kind of 'rub-a-dub' heard in the land. Real drums would throb in the market squares. This sun, which today was sparkling so beautifully and harmlessly on blue lake and white waterfall, would gleam then on cuirass and halberd, helmet and pike-point.

If the Queen lived, all would be well. The rising would wither away as other rebellions had. If the Queen died, God alone knew what would happen. England would have lost the keystone which had held the kingdom together for more than a generation. We might go back to the days of the religious struggles, back to the civil strife between the great nobles which had wasted England in the Wars of the Roses. Back . . . ? Yes, back. Whatever might be said about the old Queen – and I've come to realize in these latter years that she had many faults – at least she looked forward. England changed and grew under her hand, even though the growing pains brought many an agony. Many of the old county families hated her, and especially in the North, because she stood for the new ways and they for the old.

'Have you any money?' Kit asked very aptly, interrupting my thoughts.

'No,' I said, realizing with a shock that I hadn't a farthing. The money was with our pack-horses and merchandise, safe in Mr Bell's stable. The few pence I had carried with me were sunk, with my original clothes, in the middle of Ullswater.

'I've twopence-halfpenny,' Kit went on. 'It's not a great sum to provision two people and two horses for a ride to London.'

It wasn't. The position looked serious.

'Of course,' she said, 'if need be, we'd have to sell one of the horses. It would fetch a lot, with the lovely saddle too. Then you'd have to take the other horse and ride on. I – I'd manage somehow.'

'The trouble with you is, you've led a too sheltered life,' I told her. 'Brought up as a lady, with no one ever to question who you were or if you were honest.'

'What about the last year?' she demanded indignantly.

I ignored the interruption. 'I'm just one of the common sort,' I proceeded, 'and I know that people are not going to buy animals of this quality from boys of our age. They'd be far more likely to lock us up as horse thieves.'

Kit sighed.'I suppose you're right. We *don't* look very old or very respectable. But it does seem a shame.' She jerked her thumb at the mass of Helvellyn walling us in on our left. 'On the other side of all that, I own –'

'I wish you wouldn't go on always about what you own,' I said crossly. 'You won't own it for years yet, till you're grown up, and it's no help to us now.'

'No; but there are people living over that way who'd help me today if I knocked on their doors. They'd lend us enough to get to London, anyway.'

'Well, you can no more take our horses over that mountain than we can turn and ride back to Lonsdale – which would do just as well. We've got to keep moving ahead. We'll manage somehow.'

We had to slow to a walk, for the long pass of Dunmail Raise stretched in front of us, lifting the road between Seat Sandal and Steel Fell into Westmorland. In that nick of blue sky between the green hills they say that King Dunmail, the last King of Cumberland, was defeated and slain. But that was a long time ago, almost as long as the Romans.

On the summit of the pass we reined in and dismounted to give the horses a much-needed breather.

'No good riding them to death,' I said, sounding more casual than I felt.

'I should think not!' she exclaimed indignantly, patting the roan gelding. 'The darlings!'

'We can't afford to ride hell-for-leather, because we've no chance of getting fresh horses. So we'll have to nurse these, and get every ounce out of them.'

'Do you think we're being chased?' She glanced back. We could see the road for miles, but there wasn't a speck on it. If the pursuit had already begun, we must have drawn away from it in these first miles.

'We *shall* be chased,' I said, 'obviously. We're carrying in our heads information that means death to at least a dozen men. Do you think they'll let us go?'

'They can't catch us – not when we've got these whirlwinds to ride.'

'You're not as bright as usual, Kit. Whirlwinds tire – this sort – and we can't change them. But suppose Mr Armthwaite, or Sir Philip more likely, if he's escaped with a whole skin from my dad and the rest of them . . . suppose he's starting out after us. He's got money, he's got a name. He can pick up fresh horses in every town if he wants to.'

'And wear us down?'

'Possibly. Three hundred miles is a long way. Cheer up, though. Changing horses wastes time. If these beauties have any staying power, and if we treat them properly, we may be able to keep in front.'

I spoke as cheerfully as I could, but for the life of me I failed to see how we could treat them properly on twopence-halfpenny, even if we ourselves lived on air.

'Just a moment,' said Kit. She was exploring my saddle-bag. 'Here's a bit of luck, anyhow. Mr Armthwaite must have been planning a long ride this morning.' She fished out a bundle tied up in a white napkin. 'Here, Pete. Oat cakes! Cheese! Half a cold chicken! And – I say, a flagon of wine!'

'We'll keep that for emergencies.' It looked to me as if there were likely to be plenty of those, anyhow.

Kit hadn't finished her discoveries. 'Lend me your knife,' she exclaimed. 'I can feel something stitched into the lining.'

'Papers?' I asked hopefully.

'No. Something a dashed sight more useful!' she retorted. 'Look – money!' She held up a gold coin between finger and thumb. I saw the three lilies and the rose supporting them.

'I say! A rose-noble! Any more like that?'

'Don't be greedy, boy. Nineteen shillings and sixpence – that'll help us on a bit!'

I don't know whether Mr Armthwaite carried that

coin stitched into the lining as a sort of financial reserve, in case he found himself short when on a journey, or whether, like so many people, he believed that a rose-noble possessed special powers to ward off witchcraft. What I do feel certain of is that it could never have brought him better luck than it did to us. Nineteen and six – or nineteen and eightpence-halfpenny, as Kit reminded me – might not be a great fortune, but it would buy us all the food we wanted for ourselves and our four-footed companions.

I felt quite happy again when we remounted and cantered down the Westmorland side of the pass. Little Grasmere looked placid and reassuring under the after-noon sun; even the fantastic rocks of Helm Crag had put off their usual savagery, and the one shaped like a couchant lion looked a sleepy, friendly sort of animal.

Clop-clop . . . clop-clop . . .

On past reedy Rydal Water, through Ambleside village, to the head of Windermere . . .

We passed other travellers occasionally, and they stared to see such shabby boys so magnificently horsed. We had our tale ready if they challenged us. We were stable-lads, delivering the horses for our master. The master's name and address we varied as the miles unrolled behind us.

When we saw our first strangers approaching, I

thought of turning aside into a convenient spinney, and letting them go by without seeing us, in case they should meet our enemies farther back on the road. But, as we immediately realized, this would involve a great waste of time, and if we did it for one passer-by, we should have to do it for all. Mr Armthwaite must know perfectly well that we had taken the road to London, and there was no purpose in concealment.

'What if we went right off the road, though,' Kit suggested, 'and hid ourselves for the rest of today, and let them ride by, and miss us?'

'That *sounds* all right,' I said slowly, 'though I don't know whether we can afford to mark time for half a day.'

'No, it's no good,' she agreed. 'For another reason it'd be too dangerous. If we let them get ahead, they'll spread the story they're looking for two young horse thieves. When we move on behind them, we'll find the whole population on the lookout for us.'

And, she might have added, the conspirators liable to ride round the corner at any moment, on their way back to pick up the trail again. It wasn't likely they'd hurry on, mile after mile, once they stopped meeting people who'd seen us. The luck was against us in this – we were easy to remember, and no one on the road would have any doubt whether he'd seen us ride by or not.

All the same, Kit's suggestion set our minds working, and soon led to another idea.

'I'll tell you what,' I said, as we swung away from Windermere and mounted the low fells which sprawled across the road to Kendal.

'Yes?'

'We needn't take the obvious road to London.'

'But – *is* there another?'

'Not this side of England,' I said, with a grin. She caught on at once.

'You mean the Great North Road? You mean –'

'Yes. Turn off when no one's looking and go slap across the Yorkshire fells. It'll be hard going and we may take a bit of time over it, not knowing the short cuts, but once we're over those tops, lass, we'll be down the dales in a brace of shakes, and down the Great North Road like a lightning flash!'

'Oh, grand, Pete! While they're enquiring for us in Lancashire, we'll be half-way down the other side of England!'

'We'll hope so,' I said cautiously.

22.

Virgin Mine

I f there are two words together which have still power, after all these years, to strike a cold chill into my heart, those words are 'Virgin Mine'.

It was some little way after Kendal that we swung eastwards off the high road, choosing a deeply rutted track which looked as though it were little used save by the wagons of the district. Just before turning off, we stopped some wool merchants and asked how far it was to the next town, just on the off-chance that our question would reach other ears and mislead their owners. Then, after a careful glance before and behind, to make sure that there was no one within view to see us leave the road, we cantered off along the track. Miles away we could see the long wave of the Yorkshire fells, green-gold in the full blaze of the late afternoon.

We were lucky. We passed neither house nor man for nearly three miles, and then it was only a deaf old man sitting sideways on a cart-horse. We knew he was deaf because he asked us if we had seen a black dog, and we had to bawl in his hairy ear before we could make him realize that we hadn't, and didn't want to.

'Oo-ah,' he said amiably and rolled forward on his nag. We met no one else for a couple of miles. This was just what we wanted – lonely by-roads where there was nobody to note our passing.

'Shall we stop and eat this chicken?' I suggested.

Kit looked back over her shoulder – we'd got into the habit – but, of course, the lane behind us was as empty as usual. 'No; let's push on a bit.'

'Well, I'm ravenous. I'm going to eat something as I go.' I tore off the leg of the chicken and offered it to her. We ambled on with reins slack on our horses' necks, picking chicken-bones with teeth and fingers.

We should have to stop some time, if only for the sake of the horses. I was watching them as anxiously as a mother watches a sick baby. If one of them went lame or got saddle-galled, it would be a calamity. Even a cast shoe, in this lonely country where smiths were few, might mean a serious delay. My idea was to keep steadily on, without pushing the beasts beyond their powers. Then, if our enemies did put in an unexpected appearance at some later stage of the journey, our horses would still be in reasonably good condition and able to put on a spurt.

It was for their sakes that we decided to spend the night comfortably indoors, instead of snatching a few hours' sleep on the fell.

We came, towards sunset, to a tiny inn, high up on a shoulder of the mountains. It was, a woman warned us before we reached it, the last house we could hope to see before we landed far down in the Yorkshire dales on the other side. Ten miles, or maybe fifteen, she said, and from the tone of her voice it might have been fifteen hundred. The other side of the mountain was another world to her, as strange and remote as Africa and the Indies are to us. I think she thought us mad to be taking our horses over there, especially over such a stony pack-horse trail, but she evidently assumed that we weren't quite mad enough to make the crossing after sunset. 'You'll be staying the night at the Wool Pack,' she said in her downright Lancashire way; and Kit, rubbing herself tenderly where she felt tired of horses, said: 'Ay, mam, we'll not be going farther tonight.'

I don't suppose the stables at the Wool Pack had ever harboured two such magnificent creatures as ours. The ale-wife's husband, himself a farmer, came to gape while we groomed them and made them comfortable for the night. We spun the yarn we'd prepared – that we were delivering them to Sir Somebody Somebody at York. We chose York because we were very hazy about the towns lying opposite to us behind the wall of mountains, and we felt that most Yorkshire roads would lead sooner or later to that city. Our host was a friendly, helpful soul, and told us the landmarks to look out for the next day. When we got over the ridgeline there would be a choice of two dales for the descent. The left-hand one would lead us more directly towards York. We made a private mental note to follow the right-hand one, which would clearly veer more to the south. He also warned us against quaking bogs and chasms in the limestone. We assured him most politely that we had no intention of falling into either.

Then the stable-door was made fast, with one of his best dogs inside to give warning against horse thieves, and we went into the kitchen. The ale-wife was as friendly as her spouse. I think it tickled both of them to be entertaining two such 'young gentlemen', as they insisted on calling us.

We fairly blew ourselves out with that supper. I specially remember the ham, which in these parts is pigmeat, not mutton, as it usually is with us in Cumberland. There was a wonderful hot-pot, and a cheese as good as Mother could have made, only different, because the cheese of every valley has its own flavour, which a well-travelled man can guess with his eyes shut.

There were no other people staying in the Wool Pack that night – their guest-room was seldom used, I imagine, and then chiefly by small traders using the pack-horse trail – but in the course of the evening a number of men dropped in for their pints of ale. It was wonderful where they all came from, for there was no village near the Wool Pack, only a handful of cottages broadcast over the moor.

Shaggy, unkempt folk they were. There was a shepherd sitting in one corner with a great tankard which he sipped at slowly, never speaking to anyone. Finally he stood up, grunted something inaudible, and pushed his way out. He was more like an animal than a man.

'They get like that,' whispered the ale-wife, noticing my stare. 'Out on the hills alone, day after day, with no one to speak to, sometimes for a week at a time. They almost forget *how* to speak.'

Some of the men had grimy faces, with white staring eyeballs. Others, who had made some attempt to clean themselves, had greyish skins pitted with fine blue points.

'Miners,' said the ale-wife behind her hand. 'We've a lot of them hereabouts. It's the flying coal-dust gives them that pock-marked look.'

I noticed then how, if there was no vacant stool or settle, they squatted contentedly on their heels, with backs against the wall; and when they stood up they all had the same stooping shoulders. They got like that, I guessed, through working in the low tunnels which they drive into the banks of peat to reach the coal which lies just below the surface.

Virgin Mine . . . 'Take the left-hand trail just beyond Virgin Mine . . .' That was what the man told us. I suppose it was called that in honour of the Queen. It was the colliery where these men worked, and I heard the name often on their lips that night. It held no terrors for me then. It was a friendly, pretty name, pointing our way across the mountains to the comparative safety of the Great North Road.

We slept soundly that night, and would have slept far into the morning if the ale-wife hadn't roused us, faithful to the instructions we'd given her, at the first peep of dawn above the moor. We breakfasted quickly on porridge and mutton, paid our reckoning with the rose-noble, and rode off, our saddle-bags well packed with food for the journey.

'Remember,' she called after us from the low doorway, 'look out for Virgin Mine!'

It was a grey morning. The early scarlet had soon faded from the eastern sky, and massive clouds were piled up to hide the sun. It was fine, though. The pack-horse road was a mere ribbon of peaty mud, worming its way past mounds of heather and reedy, scummy pools. We had to go in single file, which made talking almost impossible, apart from occasional remarks shouted over my shoulder and snatched away again by the wind.

A sinister spot, if ever there was one. I sometimes wondered afterwards if Shakespeare thought of it, as we had pictured it to him when he wrote of that heath in *Macbeth*. It wouldn't have surprised me at all if we had met three witches, though morning isn't usually the time for witches to be about.

It was lucky we didn't meet any, for we'd changed our rose-noble, and I don't think a mixed handful of silver and copper is any protection against the evil eye.

It wasn't very long before we saw the colliery lying in a hollow of the moor, just aside from the track. Small black openings yawned in the hillside, and now and again you'd see a half-naked, grimy creature creep in or out, for all the world like a beetle at its hole. The coal came out in baskets, and they loaded it on sledges to be dragged down into the dales. Two men were digging on the surface itself, for here the coal measure came slanting right up, with only the thinnest covering of soil above it.

A husky giant of a man, who seemed to be directing the work, yelled to us from the side of the road, to ask if we'd seen any men as we rode along.

'Not a soul,' I said.

'They haven't any souls,' said the foreman, with bitter humour. 'Sold 'em to the Devil a while back. You mean you didn't see a man at all -- not even the one with flaming red hair you could warm your hands at?'

'Sorry,' I said.

'I think that one was in the Wool Pack Inn last night,' said Kit.

'Very likely! Drunk again, I s'pose. Good day to you!' He turned away and began, swearing horribly, to urge his men to greater efforts.

We rode on. 'Turning in about a mile,' I said; 'we must watch for it.'

'And the pot-hole – they said we'd pass that first.'

We crossed a ridge which hid the mine from view, and saw in front of us a certain drawing apart of the hills, which suggested that the dales, though not yet visible to us, were beginning to form themselves between the heights. We soon saw the pot-hole – a kind of pit in the earth ten yards to the left of the track. Its sides were of grey limestone, with the edge all fringed with beautiful mosses and clusters of bell-heather.

'Pretty,' said Kit. We'd both dismounted and led our horses closer. They seemed reluctant to come.

'Pretty?' I echoed. 'Think so?' I picked up a loose stone and tossed it down. There was complete silence while

I counted 'One, two, three, four . . .' Then there was a tiny, far-away plonk as the stone struck water.

Kit shuddered. 'Let's be getting on.'

We remounted, but we'd been riding barely a minute when a strange thing happened. I was in front, as usual, and I could have sworn that there was no living thing larger than a bird between us and the horizon. I turned my head to call something to Kit, and when I looked again there were four men standing across the track just ahead.

They made no effort to get out of our way. 'Half a moment, lad!' called one of them, flinging up his arm, and I saw that it was the fellow with the mane of filthy red hair who had been one of the company at the Wool Pack the night before.

We'd heard plenty about miners on our journey with Tom Boyd. Why the ale-wife and her husband hadn't added a warning about them to their other advice I don't know – unless it was that, depending on them for so much of their trade, they did not care to speak against them.

When I saw Red-head blocking our path, I needed no further warning. 'Look out!' I yelled to Kit. 'Ride round!' I set the example by swinging the gelding sharply to the right. But the men had chosen the spot for their ambush very skilfully, out of their deep knowledge of the moor. There was a scummy morass on the left hand of the track, which, as I had seen at a glance, was quite impassable to a horse, though a man could no doubt have waded through it. On the other side the ground was rough and hummocky, with a rivulet winding out of the morass between deep, peaty banks.

The gelding floundered. He struggled gamely. With time and without interference we should have got by. As it was, the red mane appeared suddenly beside me and an immense bare arm shot out to grasp the bridle.

I had drawn our precious pistol and cocked it. I fired now, but it was like shooting from a seesaw or a swing. From what Red-head shouted, I fancy I grazed his shoulder and hurt him considerably, but I didn't succeed in disabling him. He still held tight to the rearing horse, while with his other arm he clasped me round the waist in a great bear-hug and lifted me clean out of the saddle.

But Kit was through.

Quick-witted, and with a natural prejudice against doing what I told her, she'd ignored my advice to ride round. Instead, she dug her heels into the surprised mare and shot into those miners like a skittle-ball, hurling them right and left. Then, reining in at a safe distance, she looked round for me.

'Ride on!' I bawled before my captor extinguished me with a foul hand across my mouth.

Again Kit ignored my advice. She argued afterwards that there was no help she could hope to fetch, and in those circumstances she wasn't going to leave me. That the fate of England might hang on it did not occur to her. I'm flattered to know that, for the moment, she was thinking more of my fate.

So she rode back. Heroine or idiot? I don't know. I suppose she thought that if she'd knocked them flying once, she could knock them flying again. The black mare came thundering down all right, but this time something quite different must have happened, because before she knew what had stopped her, Kit found herself breathless on her own two feet, with her arm twisted behind her back in a grip which allowed for no argument. I looked at her dismally. I was held in a similar grip myself, and I knew it was useless to lash out at the man's shins or flail the air with my free arm.

'What do you want?' I gasped indignantly, though it was only too clear.

Red-head had scattered our money on the ground and was sorting it into four neat piles. Arithmetic was not his strong point, and he shuffled the coins several times before he could divide them to his satisfaction.

'We'll split this now!' he growled.

'You got more!' one of his friends accused him.

''Course I got more! Whose notion was it? 'Sides, I got shot at and wounded!' He patted his shoulder gingerly. A crimson stain had certainly joined the numerous other stains on his ragged shirt.

'No sense in quarrellin' over the money,' said the man who was holding me. 'There'll be plenty for all when we sell the horses. And them saddles ought to fetch something.'

'What about the lads?' asked someone.

Red-head smiled slowly and looked round at the others, as if to take their opinions first.

'Take away their pop-gun and let 'em go,' suggested Kit's captor. 'They can't hurt us.'

'Tie 'em up first, so's it'll take 'em some time to get free. Best be on the safe side.'

Red-head chuckled. 'You're right, Jack. Best be on the safe side. Always a careful one! Well, so am I. I don't mean to swing for horse-stealing, and I say, let's be on the safest side of all.'

It was all too clear what that meant. For the next ten minutes we had to stand there, facing each other in blank despair, and listening to their long wrangle. Was it safe to let us go, carrying our story to the sheriff? If not, and we had to be quietened, how could it best be done? I suppose I ought to say this for the miners – none of them seemed to fancy the task of slitting our throats.

'No need, no need at all,' said Red-head jovially. 'Not when there's that nice handy hole away back along the road.' There was a rather shocked silence at this, and I saw that the other men avoided my eyes. 'What could be neater?' went on Red-head, feeling his grazed shoulder again. There was an angry twinkle in his eyes, which were small like a bull's. 'We bury the boys – without having to harm a hair o' their heads. We'll scarcely need to lay a finger on 'em. Just a gentle push, like you might give your mate in fun . . . and there you are. And there *they* are, as you might say. No fuss, no questions, no coroner . . . As for the nags – well, if anyone asks about them, we found 'em straying on the fell, and we took charge of 'em because we felt afraid something must have happened to the owners!'

He was a persuasive man, Red-head, a born leader, and he soon won his friends to his plan. I opened my lips to speak, to make all sorts of promises and pleadings, and to tell them that Kit was a girl. But I caught a warning look in her eyes, and knew that she was forbidding me to say it. After that there was nothing to do but to pray silently for some miracle.

'Come on,' said Red-head. 'Jack, you walk along in front a bit, and watch out, just in case one o' these pedlars comes along when we don't want him.'

We waited a moment, then started behind him. Red-head held a bridle in each fist. The other two men brought up the rear, frog-marching us behind the tails of our own horses.

'You shouldn't have come back,' I muttered.

'There wasn't anything else I could do,' she said. Then she added: 'Do you think – do you think it'll hurt us much?'

I tried to comfort her. She said afterwards I talked with as much assurance as if I'd been thrown down pot-holes as a regular part of my education.

I talked desperately. Talking helped. It saved us from thinking quite so much.

We trudged on in the grip of our captors. I can remember every tiny detail of that brief walk. I can still see, in my mind's eye, the glossy hindquarters of the gelding in front of me, swinging rhythmically as one leg stepped past the other. I can see the coarse tail swishing, the neat hooves coming down so daintily, leaving each time a perfect print in the soil. I can see the eagle which sailed majestically across the steel-grey sky.

'Look,' I said, 'an eagle!'

'Yes,' said Kit.

We still couldn't realize, somehow, that our lives were over, and nothing like that mattered any more.

I remember where some blocks of limestone came cropping out of the grass, carved into strange shapes by the wind and rain. They told me that we were now within a hundred yards of the pot-hole. Just over this next hump, down in the dip beyond . . .

It was then we heard the miner named Jack, who had gone in front, running towards us and shouting to Red-head. We could see nothing ourselves, for the horses blocked our view, but we heard plainly what he said.

'Look out! Someone coming! Whole party o' men on horseback!'

'How near?' Red-head demanded.

'Just back there – and riding fast. Come on; we'd best run for it!'

'Ride for it!' said Red-head, scrambling on to the mare. He jerked her head round savagely, and turned her off on to the open moor. Jack mounted the gelding and galloped after him. Seeing themselves deserted, our two captors let go and went racing helter-skelter on the track of their friends.

'Thank God!' said Kit weakly. The miracle had happened.

We heard other voices, faint in the distance, crying 'Stop!' We heard the snap of pistols and the whine of bullets. Then came the rumble of hooves as our unknown rescuers galloped nearer.

Our joy was quickly dashed.'Look!' I groaned, as the first horseman came over the skyline. 'Sir Philip!'

23.

Terrible with Banners

He never glanced our way. He and his party were far too intent on the rough ground under them and the dwindling figures of the fugitives.

They swept across our line of vision, not a furlong from us. I heard Sir Philip shout back across his shoulder:

'They don't *look* like the boys!'

'It's the horses all right, sir!' answered the man riding next behind him. I recognized him as Mr Armthwaite's groom. Mr Armthwaite did not appear to be in the cavalcade. I suppose he had felt he was too old for such a strenuous cross-country expedition.

We watched them all vanish over the brow of the fell. I took Kit's arm and urged her to run.

'Come on! They'll never catch those brutes, but it'll keep them busy for a little while. Let's get away while we can.'

We raced away, passed the ill-omened spot where

we had been ambushed, reached the forking of the ways, and took the right-hand track.

'We'd better look out for a good place to hide,' I panted. 'We'll be getting down into the dale soon. There may be a wood.'

'What shall we do?' wailed Kit. 'We've no money, no food, no horses – nothing! What shall we *do*?'

'Don't know. Don't worry. Let's be thankful we're not down that pot-hole. Now, if only we can dodge Sir Philip, we'll have had our share of good luck for this morning.'

Kit snorted. 'What about the bad luck?'

Thinking it over later, I couldn't feel that we'd honestly had bad *luck*. It wasn't chance that the colliers had robbed us: the whole thing had been planned after Red-head's visit to the inn, when he heard of the valuable horses in the stable which we were proposing to ride across the mountain next day. And I'm afraid it wasn't chance that Sir Philip had appeared hot on our trail: with money to spend on fresh horses, and a tongue in his head to question people on the road, it was inevitable that he should pick up our scent again sooner or later. That he should come into sight when he did had certainly been good fortune. We'd never imagined we should owe our lives to Sir Philip Morton. I'd have liked to see his face if he ever learnt that, by coming five minutes later, he could have been rid of us and the dangerous knowledge we possessed, without trouble to himself!

Our road was beginning to slope steeply downwards, and a valley spread at our feet. On either side of us the fells rose, green with short turf and grey with shale. It was one of those limestone dales in which, unless there are handy crags and caves, there is no cover. The grass is like velvet and wouldn't hide a beetle. There are no trees but an occasional thorn. There isn't even – in these upper reaches of the dale – a stream to cut a way between banks. All the water is underground, bubbling away through pot-hole and cavern, till miles farther down it springs to light as a full-grown river. And you can't climb out of the dale, not quickly anyhow, because the sides go up at an angle like a high-pitched roof, with occasional terraces of sheer limestone precipice just to make matters more difficult.

There was only one thing to do. Keep on at a steady jog-trot and hope to get into different country before Sir Philip overhauled us. He must know we weren't far ahead – he would have asked at the Wool Pack, and probably at the Virgin Mine as well – and I didn't think the false scent would hold him back for long. We might have half an hour. Or at any moment now we might hear the echo of hoof-beats rolling backwards and forwards between the limestone ramparts which imprisoned us.

'Oh dear,' said Kit, 'I've got a stitch.'

'Kneel down and put your chin on your knee.'

'Ah . . . yes, that's better. All right now.'

We trotted on. Our valley was widening. It was about to enter a bigger valley. We could see fresh hills several miles in front, with a road climbing their sides. There were farms and barns, tiny cubes of grey stone, often fringed with a wind-break of firs. Down in the trough of the new, big valley were oak-woods, probably bordering a river.

'Stick it,' I encouraged her. 'Another mile or so, and we'll be all right.'

If we could reach those woods, we'd be safe from Sir Philip. That was all I cared about for the moment. What we'd do after that I didn't stop to wonder. One step at a time was plenty.

We reached a better road, running cross-wise to the rough track we had been following for so long. Instinctively we turned to our left, downhill. We were in the big valley, and only half a mile away the road ran into the gloom of the trees. There were no houses near, which was fortunate. We didn't want to be seen.

'Not much farther,' I grunted. 'All right?'

'Ye-es!' Kit was looking pale. I saw she was running

with half-closed eyes, and occasionally she stumbled over her own feet. She couldn't keep this up much longer.

The wood crept nearer. On this sunless day it looked sombre and forbidding, but to us it was a haven of refuge. A quarter of a mile now . . .

Kit stopped running and walked stiffly, holding her side. 'Have to – take it – easy – for a – bit,' she gasped. I turned my head anxiously. I was expecting to see our pursuers at any time now, but there was no sign of them on the road behind.

'All right,' I said grudgingly, and slipped my arm round her waist. She was nearly exhausted, and we fairly tottered for that last stretch. As soon as we reached the fringe of the wood she wanted to drop. I wouldn't let her. I was afraid she might do something silly, like fainting. Well, she could if she wanted to, but not just there by the roadside in full view.

'You *must* keep up for another minute,' I told her, and I dragged the poor girl through a dense thicket, a stream, and a clump of bracken before I let her collapse on a fallen log. 'Sorry,' I said, 'but there's no sense in spoiling the ship for a ha'porth of tar. Now we've got here we might as well make sure they won't find us.'

Kit managed to smile. 'I forgive you, you beast. I – I'll be better in a few moments. Do you think we're all right here?'

'Unless they get a hundred men and beat the woods from end to end.' I cocked an eye at the tree-tops. 'If need be, we shall have to climb.'

'I can do that. Listen!'

'What?'

'I thought I heard voices. There again – hark!'

I listened. There were voices, uncomfortably near, but not behind us. More to the left. Then came the loud whinny of a horse, which increased my alarm. I had thought we were well away from any place to which horses would be likely to penetrate.

'They've soon caught us up,' she hissed.

'If it *is* our old friends.' I tried to persuade myself it wasn't, but I had little ground for hope. There wasn't so many people on the road in these parts. Of course it might be men felling timber, and the horses might be there for haulage.

'Stay here,' I whispered. 'I'm going to creep along a bit and see who it is.'

I slipped away into the bracken. The voices weren't coming any nearer, but, on the other hand, they weren't receding. The speakers couldn't be far away.

As soon as I came out of the bracken on the other side I stepped almost on to the high road. I realized to my disgust that it had taken a sharp bend just after we left it, and that all the time I had been dragging

Kit (as I thought) into the trackless heart of the wood, we had actually been moving almost parallel with the road we wanted to leave.

Half a dozen horses were grazing under the trees, and I saw at once, with a heart-bound of relief, that these heavy, humdrum creatures did not belong to Sir Philip and his friends. A couple of wagons were drawn up at the roadside, and it was from behind these that the voices came. I heard every word.

> *'Lo, with a band of bow-men and of pikes,*
> *Brown bills and targeteers, four hundred strong,*
> *Sworn to defend King Edward's royal right,*
> *I come in person to your majesty –'*

Poetry in a Yorkshire wood? Was I dreaming? A new voice broke in, yet a voice which to me was old and familiar.

'No, *no*, man! You're supposed to be a baron bringing him an army, but you say it as though you were a fish-monger handing him a skate!'

That was enough. I burst cover and ran shouting between the wagons:

'Mr Desmond! *Mr Desmond!*'

They were all rehearsing on the grass-verge as I'd so often rehearsed with them. Some of the faces were new to me, but there was no mistaking that jovial visage with its comical look of amazement.

'Peter! By all that's incredible!'

I turned my head and bawled for Kit. Then, while she was still crackling her way through the undergrowth towards us, I poured out our story to the gasping company.

Desmond rose to the occasion magnificently. 'We *can* lend you a couple of horses, and welcome. Money too. But those nags of ours won't carry you much faster than you can walk. And why should you run for it?' He waved his hand at the circle of eager faces. 'Our company's more than a match for these men who're after you.'

'But they'll be armed,' I pointed out, 'and I don't suppose you've more than a sword or two and a pistol between you –'

'My dear boy, we've a positive armoury of pikes and things in the wagon! We're doing Marlowe's *Edward the Second* on this tour, and you know how many –'

'Yes,' I interrupted, 'but they're only stage weapons: they're no real good.'

'We are actors, not soldiers,' he retorted. 'Leave this to me, Peter.' He turned to the company, and clapped his hand. 'Get out the costumes. Just a helmet and a cuirass each. A pike or a halberd. Sword, too, if there's enough to go round. Not you, Nicholas or Charlie. I'll want you in your usual parts – drum and trumpet behind the scenes. Look lively everyone, or they'll be here before we are ready.'

It didn't take them long. Desmond turned to us with an excited, boyish grin, and bowed gravely:

> *'Lo, with a band of bow-men and of pikes,*
> *Brown bills and targeteers, four hundred strong,*
> *Sworn to defend our Queen Elizabeth,'*

he adapted Marlowe's lines.

'I wish there *were* four hundred of you,' I said, with a laugh. He pretended to be hurt.

'You forget I am an actor and a leader of actors! With two men and a boy I can conjure up the hordes of Tamburlaine, the Greek host before Troy, or the armies which fought at Bosworth Field. I can –'

'You'd better stop talking,' said his wife, who was looking decidedly anxious.

'Yes, my dear. And *you'd* better hide among the trees, out of harm's way.'

'No, I'll go with Nick and Charlie, and bang a drum to help them. Peter and Kit had better come with us.'

'No,' said Kit, 'we must be in this, mustn't we, Pete? Have you any helmets to spare?'

'Yes. But, look here, lads, if you're really willing to show yourselves it had better be *as* yourselves. We'll use you as a sort of bait. Come along; I'll explain the idea as we go.' He turned to the dozen or so actors. 'Double your files!' he roared, and they formed sheepishly into a tiny column. 'Smarter! *Act!* Act as if your lives depended on it – maybe they do. Forget you're rogues and vagabonds! You're not now – you're "an army terrible with banners". Look like one!'

We marched round the bend in the road, out of sight of the ramshackle wagons and the bony horses, which would certainly have spoilt the general effect. I must say that, as they warmed to the work, the actors made a good show. It was a pity there was no sun to glint on their helmets and breastplates, but I'm not sure that the dull light, together with the sombre appearance of the wood, didn't produce a more sinister result.

'The main thing is to get them dismounted,' said Desmond. 'This Sir Philip, anyhow. Then he's not so likely to make a bolt for it.' We accordingly posted ourselves on a rough piece of bank sloping up from the road. At least, Kit, Desmond, and I did, with just two of the pike-men. The others disposed themselves under cover as he directed them.

'You'd better sit on the ground at first, looking as if you were tied hand and foot,' he told us.

'Have you any cord?' I asked.

'You don't need cord. You're actors. You mime it. You show that you're tied by your faces and the way you wriggle your shoulders, not by a length of hemp. *You* shouldn't need telling that!'

The fear crossed my mind that Desmond's artistic pride might be the downfall of us all. Perhaps he didn't realize then what a grim affair this was, and thought that we, being so young, exaggerated.

We had still nearly an hour to wait before we heard the clatter of distant hooves. There could be no doubt who it was. No ordinary traveller would have come pelting down the road at that speed.

In fact, they came so fast that it looked for a moment as though they were going to sweep by without seeing our little group in the green shadows. An hour ago I would have wished for no better luck. Now I was all warmed up to gamble on Desmond's plan, and strive by a bold stroke to finish this fight for good.

Sir Philip saw us as he drew level. He slackened speed first and began in an ordinary voice: 'Have you seen – ?' Then he glanced down from Desmond's stern face to the two small huddled figures on the bank beside him. His voice went up in delighted surprise, and he pulled up his horse with a jerk which almost brought him off. 'You've *got* the scoundrels! This is splendid!' As

Desmond made no move, he slid from the saddle and came running up the bank to us.

'My name is Morton,' he said swiftly. 'Sir Philip Morton.' Desmond bowed gravely. 'These lads are wanted for horse-stealing from Mr Armthwaite, one of our Cumberland Justices.' He turned and beckoned to a couple of his companions who had reined in below us. 'I presume, sir, you would have no objection to our taking charge of them? I don't know how they come to be in your custody, but to begin with they will have to face their trial in our county, and –' He smiled pleasantly. Sir Philip could make himself immensely pleasant when he chose, otherwise he would never have brought so many men under his influence.

Desmond kept him waiting long enough for him to feel uncomfortable. Desmond, in helmet and cuirass, made a fine figure. He spoke at last, very deliberately.

'As you see, sir, I hold the Queen's commission –'

'Of course! But surely –'

'And I happen myself to be on my way to Cumberland.'

'Indeed? But an officer of the Queen won't wish to be burdened with the company of young criminals.'

'I should explain,' continued Desmond, 'that I command merely an advance-guard detachment of the army.'

Sir Philip stared. That remark had jolted him. 'May I ask what army, sir?'

'Certainly. The army which Her Majesty is dispatching to occupy the northern counties and stifle the rebellion which, we understand, has been plotted –'

'Good heavens! You appal me, sir!' Sir Philip's loyal horror was beautifully acted: it was not for nothing that he had been so keen a playgoer. 'A rebellion? Can you tell us anything more?'

'Certainly, Sir Philip Morton. You, and your friends, are under arrest for participation in the conspiracy.' It was grand to hear the long words rolled off Desmond's tongue. It would scarcely have surprised me if he had broken suddenly into perfect blank verse.

'*Arrest?* You're mad –'

'We know everything!' thundered Desmond, who hadn't even listened to half of the little we'd time to tell him.

But those words were the cue we had arranged. Desmond whipped out one of the few real pistols we possessed. Sir Philip leapt down into the road to remount. 'Come on!' he shrieked. 'There aren't enough of them to stop us! We can –'

Then he saw the six pike-men who had suddenly jumped from the wood and thrown themselves in a bristling line across the road, and the words died on his lips. He turned his head. Another rank of soldiers barred the road below. From round the bend, out of sight, came the tattoo of drums, the martial wail of a trumpet, the slow tramp of hooves.

I sympathized with Sir Philip at that moment. He saw the end as clearly in front of him as we thought we had seen it when the miners dragged us towards the chasm a few hours before. He looked down that empty road, and I don't think he saw the shadowy oak-woods or the green moors above the tree-tops. He saw the other long, dreary road which leads to Tower Hill.

'We'll cut our way out!' he shrieked again, and swung himself into the saddle. His hand went to his sword, and the thin blade was half out of its scabbard when I flung myself at his leg, heaved it sharply upwards, and toppled him over the other side of his horse.

There wasn't much fight in the others. In five minutes they were all disarmed and pinioned, without any serious injuries to either side.

'March them to the wagons, my hearties!' said Desmond, unable any longer to act as gravely as befitted an officer and a gentleman.

As we marched triumphantly round the bend in the road the drum rolled again, the trumpet sounded, and you could have sworn that a troop of cavalry was about to ride into view. The disgust on the faces of our captives

when they saw the 'army terrible with banners'! There was Nick blowing away expertly at his trumpet, so that a loud call seemed to be answered by a faint one half a mile away. There was Charlie brandishing the drumsticks and shouting orders at the top of his voice. And there was Mrs Desmond, to cap all, making the poor old cart-horses shamble round and round in a never-ending circle.

But I think the greatest shock Sir Philip had was when he came face to face with Kit. His face flamed.

'Katharine!'

'Yes, Philip.'

'You – you little vixen!'

'Think yourself lucky,' she retorted coldly. 'You might have married me.'

All of which, naturally, involved more explanations to the Desmonds and their company. And exclamations from them.

'We can't stop here gossiping for ever,' Kit pointed out laughingly. 'Remember – there's the Queen.'

That thought sobered us.

'Look here,' I said, 'if you people will look after the prisoners, and see them safely jailed, Kit and I will borrow the best of their horses and ride on. We've plenty of time; the show isn't till Saturday.'

'Saturday?' Desmond stared at me, and I saw the horror dawn in his eyes. 'Didn't you know? The date was altered – brought forward two days! *You can't possibly do it in the time!*'

In the terrible silence which followed I heard someone laughing inside one of the wagons. It was Sir Philip.

24.

A Cue Was Missed

Until now I have told this story plainly, as it happened to me, but now the time has come for me to drop out of the picture for a while and tell you what happened as it was later described to us by Shakespeare and our other friends in London.

It was Thursday evening in the royal palace at White-hall, standing out in the country beyond the Strand, nearly at Westminster . . .

All day long the carpenters had been hammering away, building the stage and the fittings which were to stand for the ramparts of Harfleur. Before they were out of the way, other men started hanging the rich tapestries which formed a background for the robes and armour of the players, and which would sweep back, when necessary, to reveal the private apartment of the French Princess. Musicians were already carrying their instruments up into the minstrel gallery, and trying to tune them in the midst of the general hubbub. Palace servants were ranging chairs for the Queen and the more important personages, stools and benches for the lesser lights who were to sit behind.

Crash! Boom!

The carpenters dropped their hammers and looked round. The palace servants turned white about the gills.

'What was that?'

'It sounded like an explosion of gunpowder!'

'Do you think Her Majesty – ?'

Burbage poked his head round a curtain. 'It's all right,' he called reassuringly. 'Just trying out the cannon effects. I think we got it a little too loud for this hall.' He turned to the head-carpenter. 'How much longer are you going to be making this racket?'

'Just finishing, sir.'

Stage carpenters always *are* just finishing. The hour of the performance draws nearer and nearer, but they can always find fresh nails to hammer or a plank to saw with an ear-splitting row. They can't hurry even for a queen. I don't think they could hurry if they were making an ark for a second Flood.

They stopped at last. The dust was swept up, the mislaid tools were discovered and carried away. Servants came and scattered sweet herbs over the floor and put fresh candles in the sconces. Burbage had a final look round before going to change. He noticed John Somers peering through the curtains. He seemed to be muttering to himself.

'Well, Somers, not sure of your part yet?'

Somers turned with a start, and a sour look spread across his sharp features. There was nothing unusual in that.

'No, Mr Burbage. I learnt my ten lines a month ago,' he said bitterly. 'Ten lines don't take much learning.'

'And you know your cue?'

'Yes, I know my cue all right. I know just what to do, Mr Burbage.'

'Well, don't despise the part because it's small. Every part is important.' Burbage walked on, and began to dress in the robes of Henry the Fifth. Shakespeare was already attired as the Archbishop of Canterbury: he went in rather for the small, older parts, like Adam in *As You Like It* and the Ghost in *Hamlet*.

'Happy about things?' he enquired.

'Oh yes; I think it will go very well. The Princess is weak, but there . . .'

'You can't expect every boy to act like Kit Kirkstone.'

'No.' Burbage donned a magnificent ermine robe. 'I wonder why they went off like that, he and the other boy. Seemed a bit of a mystery to me. Did they say much to you?'

'Not much. I fancy they had a good reason. I'd like to know how they're getting on, wherever they are.'

(Rub-a-dub, rub-a-dub, rub-a-dub . . . Drumming hooves on the Great North Road would have answered him, if we'd been near enough for him to hear.)

'Hark!' said Burbage. There was a confused murmur from the hall. 'They're beginning to come in. Not much longer now.' He called across the tiring-room. 'Everyone ready? Chorus, Bishop of Ely, Exeter, Westmorland . . . ?'

'Ready!'

An official put his head round the door and looked at Burbage questioningly. The manager nodded. A distant fanfare of trumpets, faint and sweet, heralded the approach of Queen Elizabeth. There was a last frenzied bustling behind the stage. In the hall there was a hush. Then the fanfare again, high and piercing, as the doors were flung back at the far end. The courtiers stood bowing on either side of the broad gangway. She came.

Elizabeth, by the grace of God . . .

Of England, France, and Ireland, Queen . . .

Defender of the Faith . . .

Who stopped to think to themselves at that moment that of France she did not really rule a square yard, that in Ireland the flood of revolt was beating at the walls of Dublin itself, and that the Faith she defended was no longer that for which the original title had been conferred? No; there was something about Elizabeth which silenced such thoughts when you saw her in her peacock glory.

She came sweeping down to her chair in the front row, her immense hooped skirt rising and falling on her hips, her stiff ruff framing her face, her whole body bright with jewels and powdered pearl. She looked left and right, smiling but hawk-eyed, now graciously acknowledging a bow, now making a mental note that some poor girl was overdressed or some man needed a rap over the knuckles for a fault she had remembered.

Sir Walter Raleigh walked behind her. He was Captain of the Guard then. There was Sir Joseph Mompesson, a foreign ambassador or two, lords, ladies . . . but not Sir Robert Cecil. As usual, he was at home, working late.

Elizabeth settled herself, smoothed her skirts, and signified with a nod and a movement of her fan that others might sit. There was a general rustle and scrape of feet as the Court sat down. The Chorus walked through the curtains, bowed profoundly to the Queen, and began:

> *'O, for a muse of fire, that would ascend*
> *The brightest heaven of invention!*
> *A kingdom for a stage, princes to act,*
> *And monarchs to behold the swelling scene!'*

The play rolled on. The actors strode and declaimed.
The trumpeter in the gallery sounded his flourishes.
The Queen smiled her approval and laughed at the
comedians.

In the narrow passage behind the tapestries, Burbage
bumped into Somers, and cursed him in a whisper.

'What are *you* doing here? You don't come in for
several scenes yet!'

Somers moved aside, his hand in the breast of his
doublet, and Burbage hurried by to put on his armour
for the next scene.

Somers must have slipped back immediately. I can
see him in my mind's eye, skulking in the folds of the
lofty curtains, licking his lower lip with nervousness
. . . Exeter was telling the French King:

> '. . . *Take mercy*
> *On the poor souls, for whom this hungry war*
> *Opens his vast jaws; and on your head*
> *Turning the widows' tears, the orphans' cries,*
> *The dead men's blood, the pining maidens' groans,*
> *For husbands, fathers, and betrothed lovers,*
> *That shall be swallowed in this controversy.'*

The time was near.

The scene ended. The French courtiers made their

exit, squeezing their way past Somers where he flattened himself against the curtain. The Chorus stepped on to the stage, the stage manager crouched over his cannon effects, alert and listening. Somers's hand slipped into his breast again. He, too, was listening for that cue . . .

It came. Pat followed a glorious salvo of stage artillery, which made even the Queen start in her seat and the candles flicker throughout the hall. Then every eye was on Burbage as he stepped forward, a brave figure in his armour . . .

'Once more unto the breach, dear friends, once more!'

No one had noticed anything unusual. No one had seen that sudden, convulsive agitation as John Somers was gripped in the stalwart arms of two guards and carried bodily, his cries stifled by a huge hand, into the tiring-room, where Kit and I were just beginning to breathe normally again.

The play went smoothly on. No one knew that the most important cue of all had never been taken.

25.

After the Play

T he play was over.
  I sat in the tiring-room while the actors changed and chattered round me. Burbage and Shakespeare had been summoned to receive the Queen's congratulations on the play. Kit had been spirited away by a lady-in-waiting.

'The Queen will want to see you when she hears,' Shakespeare had said. 'You can't go like that.'

'Why not?'

'Pass yourself off as a boy to Her Majesty? She'd be furious if she found out afterwards.'

'All right,' said Kit, too weary to rebel, and she let herself be led away.

I sat on, answering everyone's excited questions between mouthfuls of the first food I had tasted since dawn.

John Somers had been marched off to another part of

the palace, and Sir Robert sent for. Our work was over. All I wanted to do was sleep. But Sir Joseph Mompesson appeared at my elbow and began pump-handling my arm with the vigour of his congratulations.

'Comb your hair, and come along,' he said. 'The Queen's waiting.'

I must have looked anything but a young hero as I tottered through the palace beside him, for my knees were weak and I could scarcely stand upright after so many hours in the saddle. I was thankful when we came to a door with two halberdiers in front of it.

Four people looked up as we entered: the Queen, Sir Robert Cecil, Sir Walter Raleigh, and a girl in a flame-coloured skirt and bodice, whom I did not recognize for a moment, but who must (I knew) be an extremely important and favoured personage, for she was sitting beside the Queen.

'Peter Brownrigg, Your Majesty!' said Sir Joseph, and I knelt to press my lips to the gnarled old hand extended to me. The brown fingers were knobbly with too many rings.

'You may take a stool, Peter Brownrigg,' said a brisk voice above my head. 'It's not good for young people to sit about too much, least of all in the presence of their sovereign; but I understand that you and this girl have been at some pains to prolong my weari-some existence.'

As I sank on to the stool which someone pushed forward, I realized that the young beauty in the flame-coloured dress was Kit. My jaw dropped. Not even on the stage, not even as Juliet, had I ever seen her looking like that. Was this Court lady the Kit I knew? She must have guessed what was going through my mind, for, as the Queen turned to whisper something to Sir Walter, Kit smiled encouragingly at me. I saw the candles dance in her eyes, and I knew then that she was still the same.

We told our story then, much as I have told it here. The Queen exclaimed loudly at several points and swore when we began to list the names of the conspira-tors. Sir Joseph slapped his thigh when I described my escape from Ullswater, and I saw that in his mind's eye he was following every step I had taken that evening on Helvellyn. Even Sir Robert broke silence to join in the laughter when we told of Sir Philip's capture.

'He shall be dealt with,' the Queen promised grimly. 'And then you rode straight here?'

'It sounds as though they *flew*,' said Sir Walter.

'It's well they didn't dawdle,' retorted the Queen. She turned to Kit. 'Nice goings-on for a young girl! Very unladylike! Gallivanting about the country on

stolen horses disguised as a boy! Scandalous! Well,' she barked, 'what have you to say for yourself?'

Kit blinked under this unexpected attack. Then she sat up straighter, so that her cropped head showed funnily against the snow-white cambric of her ruff.

'Your Majesty, there are no words better than your own: "Though I have the weak body of a woman, I have the heart and stomach of a man!"'

The Queen laughed her harsh laugh, till her ear-rings shook. 'Well answered, Miss Impudence. Though, God help me, it's a far cry since the day at Tilbury when I said that. Ah, well . . .' She sighed. 'But it won't do as a general thing, you know. Mind that, Robert – find your spies elsewhere, not in the nursery!' I could see Kit boiling at that. Elizabeth went on:

'Your guardian doesn't seem to have taken very good care of you, child. We must alter that. I've a fancy to make myself your guardian. Would you like to be a ward of the Crown, eh?'

'If I *must* have a guardian,' said Kit tactlessly.

The Queen tapped her cheek with her fan. 'Only for a year or two, child. You'll give me as much trouble as Ireland, I don't doubt. Soon you'll be old enough to choose a husband, and I'll be rid of you.'

'I don't want one, Your Majesty.'

'You will, you will. Just wait. And – you may go

farther and fare worse.' She swung round to me. 'And what can I do for you, boy? At this moment, I mean.' And her wicked old eyes swung back to Kit with a meaning which made us both go scarlet. 'Well,' she went on, 'don't you crave a boon, boy? People always crave boons when they serve their sovereign. Eh, Walter? What's it to be? Make it reasonable. I'm a poor woman.'

I looked at her. What *did* I want? We Brownriggs have always been simple statesmen, holding our land from the Crown, beholden to nobody. We have never sought wealth or honours – your true statesman will not take even a knighthood. We have farmed our fells, and held our land against all comers, asking no favours.

I cleared my throat. 'Your Majesty,' I said, 'there are some common lands which have been ours and our neighbours' from time immemorial. Sir Philip stole them and enclosed them for himself. Will you hand them back to us, and confirm us in possession of them for ever?'

She stared at me. Then she turned to Sir Robert with a chuckle. 'I think we might grant this boon, eh? After all, it won't cost us anything.'

So it was that Sir Philip's wall went down even before his head under the axe on Tower Hill.

What else is there to tell? Only that the Queen proved a shrewder prophet than we, and lived to send us a wedding gift. As I lay down my pen, I look through the fine glass window across the silver mirror of Ullswater, and hear from the garden the shouts of laughter as Kit shows my sons how to climb the apple-tree.